Unpublishable

Acknowledgment is gratefully made to the contributors for permission to print the material for the purpose of this anthology.

Published in the United States by:
Archway Editions, a division of powerHouse Cultural Entertainment, Inc.
32 Adams Street
Brooklyn, NY 11201
e-mail: info@powerHouseBooks.com
website: www.archwayeditions.us

Library of Congress Control Number: TK

ISBN 978-1-57687-971-9

Printed by Friesens Corp.

First edition, 2020

10 9 8 7 6 5 4 3 2 1

Printed and bound in Canada

Design intern: Emily Bluedorn
Interior layout by Robert Avellan
Book design by Francesca Richer

ARCHWAY
EDITIONS

Unpublishable

**Edited by Chris Molnar
and Etan Nechin**

Archway Editions, Brooklyn, NY

CONTENTS

8 Unpublishable

INTRODUCTION

What was Unpublishable?

It began with the reading series at Columbia University's MFA program, called Gallery. Infrequent and hidebound, few students ever got the chance to read. We decided to start an Ungallery at POWERHOUSE Arena, where Chris worked, to make a series inclusive of different styles and voices and implicitly against the academy.

After graduating, we wanted to continue what had been a successful series while breaking out of the Columbia scene. Etan recalled how in Tel Aviv genres were rarely siloed, how arts events were always unpredictable and exciting in a way that readings never are in America. Using these ideas we created Unpublishable, based around the idea that any artist has work which they love but cannot publish, for any number of reasons: a genre they've never worked in before, offending of sensibilities (although always in good faith), impossible to place for publication, the eternal struggle of the unknown author or simply a style that the world hasn't yet lit on as great.

As we canvassed for writers, the response went far beyond what we expected. James Cañón brought a brilliant piece about an acquaintance, Soberbia, whose permission he had never received and now couldn't find. Jean Kyoung Frazier read from her character-building practice writing. Steve Anwyll practically broke the series with his searing, controversial piece, which Bud Smith later said he'd tried to make him edit but couldn't. A surprising number of writers were insulted by the idea that anything they would write could be called "unpublishable," which certainly says something about them—what exactly is unclear. Bud said his outlook is that anything is publishable; fitting his beautifully optimistic nature, but not ours. Eileen Myles found something for us that had only been published in translation—and read it at the Poetry Project instead, keeping our antiestablishment (possibly even anti-antiestablishment) cred intact.

The events themselves were one of a kind, never to be seen again. Hratch Arbach's combined reading and video cannot be fully replicated here, let alone the installments of the Wild Radio series that Chris projected with Brent Kite. The uproar around Steve's piece and his subsequent reading under the Manhattan Bridge. Mary Boo Anderson's timed Tweetstorm. Phyll Pope reading John Farris. Mina Hamedi and Naomi Falk's specially written, uncategorizable piece; hampered by a broken PA in front of a packed house, now reprinted here in full. We originally wanted musicians, scientists, artists—but settled for just the most eclectic group of writers we could gather.

Now with the series safely in the rear view, we can already take credit for being an incubator. 2020 brought thrilling debuts from Jean, Arash Azizi, and Jameson Fitzpatrick. Chris Gonzalez has his coming out in 2021. Chris and Nick Nicoludis founded Archway Editions, which will now be publishing John Farris' last poems. Mina Hamedi is an agent for Janklow & Nesbit. James Cañón found Soberbia.

And of course, now they're in print, right here at your fingertips. Maybe Bud Smith was right after all. In true Unpublishable form, the nature of these works remains provisional; defying logic; everything that is unpublished should be published and vice versa. This is writing from the margins that is becoming integral. And of course once these authors have taken over, it will be time for a new Unpublishable to rise up.

What If Everyone Had To Tell The Truth About Themselves?

Jean Kyoung Frazier

I'm a big beautiful man with big beautiful muscles. I have a big finance job and make big fat stacks of cash that I use to buy cocaine, hookers, and pressed juices. I love finding creative ways to say that I went to Harvard and that I have not one Porsche, but two, and an Audi, like the one Iron Man drives. Once, I met Mischa Barton and she told me I was hot and I said, No thanks, babe. Every morning, I cry in the shower.

I'm a thirty-eight year old stay-at-home mom who looks twenty-five. It's a great source of pride for me when I go to the liquor store and the clerk asks to see my ID. I have a husband who also looks twenty-five and we look so good in our daily Instagram posts. Our two kids, older boy, younger girl, seven and five, I already know that they will also become gorgeous adults that will marry other gorgeous adults. All my friends are jealous of me and I love inviting them into my home to see all their jealousy in one place. I can't stop fucking people who aren't my husband. My yoga instructor, the manager at my favorite farm to table restaurant, my high school Calculus teacher, the UPS and Fedex driver—I worry they are all in love with me and will one day tell my husband about the alleyway handjobs and the back-of-car ass fucking. Sometimes, I puke up meals from the stress of it all.

I'm a corporate tax lawyer. I am the youngest partner in company history. My hairline shows no signs of receding. I have a very strict diet and run every morning. I'm really boring at parties. When I walk into a room, I watch people look at me and then quickly look away. If you are unfortunate enough to be stuck next to me at a party, you will struggle for several minutes to try and come up with questions that will get me to provide answers interesting enough that will allow you to say something interesting back—"So, how is work?" "It's good," "Have you seen that new movie, the one with the beautiful young woman and the slightly attractive older guy?" "No," "Well, what about the TV show with—" "I don't watch TV either," "Oh, okay, well are you doing anything this weekend?" "No,"—I have no hobbies. I wake up, run, go to work, come home, maybe run some more, maybe just go to sleep, I never have any dreams. I am doing well, but sometimes when I'm sitting in my desk chair looking out my window at the streets below, running along cracked sidewalks in the day's first light, I think about how nice it would be to have friends. I wonder what it would be like to get a call from someone who doesn't want anything from me but to hear my voice. Being in love sounds nice too. How lovely to come home to someone and fall asleep in their arms.

I'm a sophomore in high school in a small Midwestern town. I have straight A's and friends to sit with at lunch, am a part of various clubs and a varsity athlete, other parents tell my parents how charming I am—I'm what you would call well-adjusted. Everyone tells me how great it is to be young, that I'm so lucky to be the age that I am, how thrilling to have my whole life ahead of me. I like to go driving late at night along the empty single-lane country highways flicking my headlights on and off. I know it's dangerous, but I can't stop wondering if there's such a thing as free will or if my whole life has already been decided for me. I flick those headlights off and I can't see anything in front of me, don't know anything except that I'm barrelling forward at high speed and what will be will be. My boyfriend and I are saving ourselves for marriage, but I don't think he would want to save himself for me if he knew that I masturbated in bathroom stalls after every period. That I don't think of him, but of the point guard on the girl's basketball team and the way sweat drips down her body, how at practice I think about running over to her and sucking on the wet spots of her jersey. I am disgusting and I shouldn't be anyone's wife, shouldn't pass along my genes to another generation. The longest I have driven without headlights is twenty-seven seconds.

I'm an old woman in a nursing home. I could tell you my age, but does it matter? All you need to know is that I'm old and I can't wipe my own ass and I've seen a lot. I've lived through wars, watched people that used to be spit on, celebrated, parades thrown in their honor, seen women, my own daughters, and granddaughters, achieve more than I was ever able to dream, I really liked the iPhone, emojis were everything I didn't know I wanted. I've had a full life, a beautiful life—I feel like such a piece of shit for being angry that I will die soon. I hate anyone that is even a day younger than me, anyone that has more time left than me. My kids visit with their kids and I hate them. I hate them for their life and mostly, I hate myself for causing them to waste that life at my bedside. I think the Inuits got it right— the best thing to do with the elderly is to send them off on a piece of ice and let them die at sea before they get much chance to think about their lives and everything they never got to do.

I'm a young artist living in the greatest city in the world—you know which city I'm talking about. I write spare short stories, play bass in a punk band called something that shows how progressive and anti-establishment we are, I mostly paint large canvases dark, moody colors and piss all over them, name them after everything I've eaten and drank that day—I am sure someone will buy one soon. I live in a shitty studio apartment with no AC, no TV, but sometimes

I watch the cockroaches run along the walls and think about how I have never had a sexual experience sober. My parents are dead and I have no siblings. I feel pretty good most days.

Erin Taylor

please delete me
weed is the only thing that makes me feel good rn

no one ever wants to hear about a pedophile father
        when the man who asked for no marks (think of his
                                                    wife)
            told me he sniffed the panties of the barely blooming
            my whole body became anchored to
            my barely blooming self first learning the word
                molestation

and how those who are barely alive shouldn't know anything
            of bad men and what they do.

                    I've carried around bad men my entire life,
                    thanklessly,
                            they still call me on my birthday
                            show up at my job I am still just
                        a child without control
                        over my own circumstances.
        the man who doesn't want marks
        let me piss on him,

                    it would have felt like a victory if he didn't enjoy it
so   much.

I have a full day of doing nothing to look forward to
    I don't believe in a "work culture" because it implies
  a belief in "work"
        a belief in capital, a subtle justification
        of poverty of wealth of cops

        if I ever work in a coworking space, shoot me
            I want to find a dynamic solution to the end of
            everything we know right now

after therapy I went to the earth room and thought of
a world after us

        a world where every dollar bill is turned into mulch
        and every home overgrown

the Russian baths welcome us into spring
along with the news, the news is always so much
and in our face and make cowards of us all.

spending all my days in a dungeon of my own
creation, I let the wax fall onto his nipples
drip drip drip a little nipple slut

he moans about something insignificant,
I am envisioning myself on an island
where the only men that exist are collared.

men should be seen not heard,
it would be horrible if they didn't want it so much.
I want to embrace my dream of

waterboarding an old white man.

well acquainted with evil men
a mythical goodness exists in
this trump era, a splendid ignorance
to suffering.

I feel on the edge of humanity,
a technological fuckfest. there is no
longer an escape from our own
touch. the melting of the ice isn't
even talked about anymore, only degrees.

nyc is a beautiful place to fall in love.
I want to have a mortgage in an apartment
that will be underwater in twenty years
with you.

Game

Noah LeBien

one day
in the long off ago
child they called us bitch and fag
till i was petrified if that makes you
emotionally reaching out, plucking black squirrel
genitals from a branch, always giving good head
to others and playing the girlfriend
for straight boys, the lamentable grace
        their aggression concealed
black striped panties, eggshells in a black garbage
bag crawl into my mouth while i'm sleeping
and our ankles burst open
like the mouths of trout as we
scald into the night with our skateboards
and all the things we whisper are just
a game that never fails nor succeeds, so American
indebted to how
it puts a tracer beam
into the pupils of manchildren
like cranberry bread, with all the rest of us here
terrified, clinging to the edge
of the iris we saw as lawnflowers

Hivemind

everyone is aching right now
    but i make it so
        with my cock like an angler fish
            issuing out of the gloom
                is how we make food
      for the Borg of our pathetic time existence
      yes, we are living in shame
      too and share even that
    there are no alternate dimensions
without the emptiness of the universe
      and dissimilation from the hive mind
           which is not
                identity really, just more loneliness
                that all possibilities
            have enough of
              making $$$
        to do more that i
        can't stand about myself   i'm *in it*, i'm this thing
    here, beauty and emptiness meet
  with a chord around its mouth and the feeling that
i'd kill for sleep, i'd sleep on a bed of nails for sleep
           o sleep, give me yourself   giving is assimilation
           assimilation is species   species is sex-sleep
           one gives oneself back   potential for giving
           equals potential for sleep   for love and abasement porn
                O galactic network,
    an escape from this immense, impossible individuality
            gleaming like fish roe on the infinite, unscrolling

underbelly of the Deep Web deep-dive
with nothing makes sense   anymore and i forget
how even we got here and what
our message to you
even was, why we came
but we are alive, know it
and just because   i'm here on the other
side of this screen doesn't mean
the confusion you cannot
guess at behind my eyes   does not complete you

Hauntology

there once was a lavender color : it passed over your face
so light it was : a whisper from another universe

which is what inspired you : eyes open we lay in the broken glass
blood poured upwards in huge, silent swathes : for hours and hours

and you described what you saw of the footage : you dug crust out
of the dials which made your heart stop : it was there there under
the pyre

that i loved you : a choice to be what you are not now but
could have been before : which is the true future, believe it

and don't be frightened, this is to celebrate you : i deserve above all
else to watch you squirm as the procession of cake-full mouths : spit
into your lap, lab coats smoldering

but the statistics are out of date, the laboratory is abandoned : the
reactor is shut down lead paint-chips, sheet metal crackling : the
occasional sputtering helicopter

and this is the prairie : the wind on your bare shoulders
the hush of the tall grass : the sunset, the wheat

your body is a void, an absence, there is no path : here is my portal
here is my unexplained phenomenon : i will grant your one wish

Tehran, Cairo, Tel Aviv: Iranian Communist Perspectives on Israeli Independence and Anti-Imperialist Unity (1951–52)

Arash Azizi

"We congratulate the Israeli nation on the third anniversary of Israeli independence on behalf of the Iranian Jewish community. We salute the spirit of martyrs and freedom-lovers who lost their lives in this path. We hope that the Israeli nation is able to achieve greater success and victory as its fruitful struggles go on."

Such were the thundering words of an editorial by *Bani Adam*, the weekly newspaper of the Cultural and Social Society of Iranian Jews (CSSIJ), on May 4, 1952. While *Bani Adam* was produced by Iranian Jews and it primarily addressed them as its audience, its title shows a particular bent and a broader audience in mind. Taken from a famed couplet by the Iranian poet Saadi, '*Bani Adam*' means the 'human-kind' and it evokes the anti-racist message of human solidarity that the couplet carries. The CSSIJ and *Bani Adam* both belonged to a plethora of organizations and media outlets that were allied with the Iranian communists of the Tudeh Party.

In the first few years after the foundation of the state of Israel in 1948, the Iranian communists attempted to put forward a unique perspective on the new state of Israel and the anti-imperialist struggle of its neighbors in the Arab world and beyond. Many elements of this unique perspective might be perplexing or surprising to contemporary readers: communists of a Muslim country advocated hard for their country to officially recognize the state of Israel. They praised the Israeli victory in the war of independence and maintained that the real enemy had been British colonialism and its Arab partners, not the Arab people whose fate was intertwined with that of the Jewish masses. Just as the first shots of the Cold War were being fired, the Iranian communists attacked the US for being too beholden to its Arab allies and not sufficiently pro-Israel just as they called on the new state to ally itself with the rising anti-colonial forces of the Third World.

Changes on all sides would soon make such a perspective obsolete. But this paper is not focused on what was to come later. Instead, my aim is to elucidate the position of Iranian communists in the early Cold War era. This era is one of 'lost voices' in many senses. The canonized versions of Cold War history have erased the fluidities and intricacies of the politics of these early years in favor of straightforward and teleological accounts written from the perspective of hindsight. But in the early years of the Cold War, positions that were to become rigid in a few years were much more fluid and open to change. There were, for instance, no harsh demarcation lines between social democracy and communism; no strict binaries when it came to supporting the Soviet Union. Same is true when it comes to Zionism and the State of Israel. While anti-Zionism and a very critical take on the State of Israel was soon to become a hallmark of the far left in the Muslim Middle East—and indeed much of the globe—things were different in the early 1950s.

Fight like an Egyptian

In December 1951, the Middle East was going through a tumultuous time and the order that the colonial powers had enforced on the region in the aftermath of the First World War was challenged on numerous sides.

It was in such a political atmosphere that *Bani Adam* made an intervention in an editorial on December 16, 1951."To achieve liberation from the fetters of colonialism, the nations of the Middle East must work together," the editorial's headline suggested. What makes *Bani Adam*'s perspective unique is the place of Israel in this scheme. The editorial starts with praising "the Egyptian nation for its heroic actions" which it saw as similar to "admirable success that the Iranian nation has achieved in this path." As the journal attacked the "old and decrepit colonialism of Britain and its Western allies," it reminded the readers that it was "the Israeli nation who rose three years ago to cut short the hand of British predators." Offering its unique perspective on the 1947-48 war, *Bani Adam* wrote: "The Arab nations, without any benefit to themselves, were provoked against the Jewish nation. Innocent people killed each other in vain. The Arab and the Jew, who had a common enemy, started fighting each other to death due to the conspiracies and deceptions of that very enemy. At the end, however, the British government failed in bringing about its colonial plot and had to concede defeat faced by the will of the heroic people of Israel."

Jewish Iranian communists were in a unique position when calling on the Israeli state to adopt an anti-US and anti-colonialist position. Not accepting the Zionist ethos that considered them as not properly Iranian, they proudly declared their allegiance to both the world Jewry and the Iranian nation. "We address the ruling class of the Israeli nation toward its grave duties both because of the love that we have for the life of our co-religionists in Israel and for the people of the Middle East as a whole, who we consider ourselves to be a part of," *Bani Adam* said.

Audacity of fraternity

The pages of *Bani Adam* during the years of 1951 and 1952 are filled with similar analysis. The consistent position of this communist outlet was to defend the Soviet Union and its international line, urge the Iranian government to officially recognize the state of Israel, introduce news of Israeli progressives to the Iranian audience and to enjoin on the Israelis to join hands with liberation movements in the region. In short, it strove to build an anti-imperialist fraternity that'd cut across all religious, sectarian and national lines.

Bani Adam thus worked patiently and consistently to present its vision of anti-imperialist fraternity from Tehran to Tel Aviv to Cairo against all odds. In those early days of the post-war era, it dared to imagine a Middle East consisting of sovereign anti-colonial nations that would drive the European colonialists and the US imperial interests out. In this vision, Israel had a place as a progressive, anti-colonial nation and Jews of other countries were seen as equal nationals of their own countries who needed to defy the Zionist logic by fighting for justice and democracy in their own countries while maintaining ties with their fellow Jews in Israel.

Demise of a vision

Changes that defeated the vision of *Bani Adam* came on all sides. The Israeli state, under the leadership of Ben Gurion, increasingly strengthened its pro-US bent in the Cold War. Leftist forces like Mapam who had a significant Arab membership started a rightward drift that would have them more or less absorb themselves inside the ruling social democrats. Thus, a politics like that of *Bani Adam* would have found no significant partner in Israel. In the Soviet Union itself, Stalin started an anti-Semitic campaign in his last year in office.

Maintaining of a significant Jewish-Israeli communist voice became increasingly difficult and after the 1965 split, the Israeli Communist Party was almost entirely limited to Israeli Arabs. As such, there was scarcely room for an optimistic, universalist, anti-imperialist vision like that of *Bani Adam* in 1951.

The tragic demise of this vision had consequences that were not limited to the Israeli-Palestinian issue. Years later, in January 2012, in a BBC Persian panel on the history of the Tudeh Party, Farhad Farjad, a central committee member of the party in 1970s, lamented that a party that had once openly called for diplomatic recognition of Israel would come to take reactionary positions. It is noteworthy that Farjad saw the mentioned pro-Israeli position as symbolizing the golden age of Tudeh Party. For people like Farjad, the honor of communism had been tarnished when it ceased to stand for such progressive universalism; just as for thousands of Israeli citizens, the honor of their state had been irreplaceably tarnished when its promise of anti-colonial fraternity with Arabs had repeatedly turned out to be hollow.

Gas Stations at Night (Radio Remix)

Brent Kite & Chris Molnar

One
            [turning the dial

                  looking for something they'll never find]

Locked into distance
Every step falling
Tender reminder
Gas Stations at Night
Sitting in silence
Lost in reflection
Rainbow in oil now merging in
     white ink blank paper
Dry rot at Days Inn
     room moved into an empty room

Dwelling in distance

Oasis in silence

     don't even know what to want

000000000
OOOOOOOOO
ooooooooo   Sine-Aid

the sinus medicine
in the bright red box

see who will see me standing here
standing here what
will i see

Look inside the look of falling

of falling
like radio

dead air across
dark America

and wasn't the end
what we passed
on the road
some miles back

THE RAIN DROPS AWAY IN SOUND JUST GIANT FLOP-
PING BEADS SILENTLY HURTLING THROUGH CLOUDS
SOME INABILITY TO MAKE AUDIBLE NOISE TO CONNECT
THE MOST MYSTERIOUS MUSIC I AM TRYING TO USE
UP ALL THE GAS IN THE CAR THE WHEELS WON'T GO
QUICK ENOUGH WE ARE DRIVING AND DRIVING AND
DRIVING GHOST VOICES SPEAK UNORGANIZED WORDS
MEMORIES SCRUBBED OUT A GHOST CITY WITH UNOR-
GANIZED TREES AND HOUSES AN ISLAND IN THE RIVER
WITH A FIRE BLAZING AS WE CROSS THE BRIDGE I CAN
SEE PEOPLE WE KNOW DANCING AROUND IT THERE IS
A COMPLETE FEELING OF SPACE AND NOTHINGNESS

ABOVE THE RAIN THERE ARE NO CLOUDS AT ALL

Gas Stations at Night

> *wind*

Render reminder

> *rising remember*

Ember reminder

> *sky above, great wind*

Lot to take in

> *motel for two voices*
>> *time to be ready this time*

Artifacts of the Moon

By Brent Kite & Chris Molnar (with Wyllis Cooper)

1.

"Music by Claude Thornhill, his piano, and his orchestra…"

"A very pleasant good evening, ladies and gentlemen. The American Broadcasting Company presents from coast to coast music by Claude Thornhill, his piano, and his orchestra, playing for dancing in the Café Rouge at the Hotel Pennsylvania, another Statler Hotel here at 34th St. and 7th Ave. in New York City. This evening we'll hear songs by Fran Warren and Dean Williams. Here's our first song, a fine instrumental arrangement by Claude Thornhill and the orchestra, figure it out for yourself, Robin's Nest.*"*

2.

"Ahh, shut up. Why can't people let me alone?"
"Yeah? Yeah, yeah, I'll see ya. I'll see if I get an idea. I've no more idea than a rabbit."

3.

Who knows how much I love you?
You do…
No one means more to me than you do…
You take December and smile it into May
And then December comes back again

When you're away

Who has a charm that very few do?
Who makes life necessary?
You do…

4.

"Come on in, I said!"

5.

"You ever look through a big telescope? At the sky at night. At the things up there. Things so far away you sprain your brain just trying to imagine how far away they are. With nothing between you and them, billions and billions of miles of nothing. I don't know what it does to you but brother I freeze. Listen, do you know there are holes in the sky? No, I mean it, I've seen them. There's a thing in the constellation Andromeda, no no wait a minute, I'm not going to get technical with you, just listen. There's this thing, astronomers call it the Horsehead Nebula, you know what it is? It's a hole. It's a great big patch of nothing. Just nothing. There aren't any stars there, there's just a hole. No, nobody knows anything about it, astronomers look at it, take pictures of it, and there it stays. There it is now and tomorrow and the next day, and a million years from now, and it's been there always. Yes it has! It's so far away, that what you see now is the way it looks is the way it looked a billion years ago. Before there was anybody to see it then. And there's lots more of those things…"

6.

I have it on the utmost authority
Alien voices
caught in dust storms
The taste of cheap wine

The tidy and anonymous room

And I can begin to hear
silence and wind
the tall spark of desire
is all that creates
in a void

Fighter jets fly over the mountains
through space unfathomable
mirrors in the desert
a wild massive baby
weaned on sun
the smell of wet chaparral
under soft feet
crushed small timbers
the slightest spark
of unknown desire

The taste of chemicals
empties me down to need

Everything is in unstoppable slow motion
until I arrest myself
on the utmost authority
presenting firm lines
to slide through
a wild massive baby
a compromising roar
mirrors in the desert
filled with coiled desire

The taste of mortar

and bricks in the sun

I have it on the utmost authority
Unusual stars
from behind the Paiute wall.
Alien constellations
life of gargantuan flesh.

…oh what do I find
I knew you well
Once I held you in my arms
Once I thrilled to all your charms
You loved me too

7.

That's what you said
But was it true
You're only one in a million
You're only one if you play
But I learned just what the blues meant
When you went away
I knew you well
We were lovers long ago
Now you're someone I don't know
So you forgot
I can't forget
I knew you well

"7 o'clock in the morning, the fog was hanging in the sky like, like a velvet curtain, you couldn't see a streetlight a block away. And when I fumbled around under the table where I'd left her, she wasn't there. I found a paper of matches finally. She wasn't there! You think you know what terror is?

Well, don't let me tell you! I stood up at last and, and the night was so still I could hear the foghorn from way up toward Point Doom. The fog as I told you was thick as, well, my glasses were taped, there they were the two of them, and there wasn't any fog in the picture, I couldn't mistake them, I fell to the curb, and together they raised their hands and beckoned to me, I knew I couldn't move, but I opened the door, and I went down the steps in the fog, and there was just one tiny step in the fog, just one tiny step, and I knew they wouldn't be there…"

8.

"Oh no, oh no. I didn't go to sleep permanently. I woke up. You guess what time. I didn't sleep anymore. I sat up and smoked cigarettes. I like the house. I see the picture. She lit kerosene lamp, and there it was. Right? I should have stayed. Rag carpet on the floor. A pot near the kitchen sink that went ee-wah ee-wah when she dropped the water for the coffee. You know there wasn't a few cans in the kitchen cupboard…"

9.

"Okay, okay, so I'm a chump."

"I don't like the stars up above us. I don't like the lights down below. I don't like the silence. All I can see is two black shapes in front of me. Blacker shape, that's the building with nothing in it."

10.

"Wait! Wait for me!"

"Across the little trestle, away from the door he closed on my friends, through another door into a long shed in the dark. And I was glad I couldn't see the stars. Out another door at the end of the shed. On the path past the celostep reaching up the sky shining in the starlight. Looking like one of those visitors from Mars you heard about on the radio. Across the little

wooden bridge with the two with the two eyes in the hundred-inch dome staring down at me and a cold wind coming down the mountain. Up the ramp, into the tomb itself. And up the iron stairs."

"Follow me."

"A little yellow stairs at the head of the stairs, and then out on the catwalk in the dark with the floor forty feet below us. Up another ladder, my legs are getting tired."

"Up! Follow me,"

"Up another dizzy ladder! And another! And across another spidery walk!"

"Here, sit in this seat."

This isn't the street I thought I turned into
Here in Pleasant Prairie, down on Corporate Drive
Everything is so uncertain in them
Keep your eye
slightly off focus
Always happens just a little before you're ready
Want to be suspended in beautiful nowhere

Operator, that line is still folded
Have I a womb for mystery
Wave me over the flatlands, I'm sliding on radio
I emptied my breath on the radio
So glass and china
Will be cleaner and whiter
Like when you look at your hands in a dream
Teeth snapping fresh I crawled in the alphabet
Hollow compared to something seen

One word, look outside your window

Describe what you see
Closer and
Closer and
Closer
Nothing but dustheaps nearby, where we left them
Flyers for a missing cat, opening the puzzle pages
Found a circle, rain sounds like everything
Learned to stop moving
Only thing I knew to do was fall asleep

11.

Start with what we lost, then list expenses
Itemized encounter found you twisting under shadow
Stuck in the song in its groove
Silver smoking train ran round
Night crept into the barn
Certain of finding the missing compartment
Hidden in the eye of the echo

Strange, something changed in the rerun
Ground of static rising, patterns of bees in the air
Singing through cellophane
One one one one one
One day you'll see where you're standing
Speak quickly now
Forget the time and place
Where was your face when you lost it

I can't see, can't get to sleep
Orbits my cloud like a gnat
Something forgotten and try to remember
Some seasonal festivity

The time of unpeeling
No comfort in these shells

Than light across the parking lot
To sit and respond in the brilliance of the moment
Than signal in the network
No more real am I
Please ask a specialist
to view your erasure
Who can tell me
What was lost

Please respond care of
Space between the office park
Where the grass is boundless

12.

(   )

(why i didn't bother) saying goodbye

Kate Olsson

When Dave is here everything is wrong. The kitchen sink is full of crumbs, the whole house smells faintly of melting plastic, and the toilet paper rolls are all on backwards. His presence is loud for that of a man who rarely speaks: he sleeps in the living room to the local news station blaring, texts on his flip phone through every meal, the volume of his keypad turned all the way up, all the while he is there, enormous, unmoving, taking up space and atmosphere at the dinner table or on the couch.

Dave is my stepmother's brother, an uncle of sorts, I guess, but to me, really he is nothing. When he stays with us it is out of necessity, the result of a fumigation, or resignation, or eviction notice. I used to ask why Dave had to stay with us all the time. Did he not have friends? But my dad and Sheila would just shrug and say something along the lines of, "He's family," because when you're as old as they are I suppose that seems like reason enough.

Mostly, I just try not to be home. Dad and Sheila are busy people, so they tend not to notice. I ride my bike to Michaela's and together we ride to the skate park behind the local branch of the library.

"Some kid shot himself in the head right there," a boy in knee-pads and elbowpads but no helmet is telling me. He is pointing at the ground right under my bare feet with the hand that isn't holding his skateboard.

"No way," I tell him, but I take a step back, just in case. "There'd be a stain in the concrete, or something."

"Powerwashing, man," the boy says. "They get the fire department out here with their hoses." He mimes holding one up, imitates the sound of gushing water and laughs lazily, in the way that, combined with his helmetlessness—and probable drug use—spells brain damage.

I look away from him over to the top of the half-pipe, where Michaela is sitting with a guy named Toby, legs dangling.

Toby, well, he is the reason we are here, the reason I am here, talking about the logistics of removing carnage from concrete with fire hoses instead of watching TV on Michaela's couch and eating junk while her mother chain smokes and talks on the landline in the kitchen.

Michaela's blonde hair is flat-ironed, except for one wavy section she missed in the back I've decided not to tell her about. It's falling across her face and she is laughing too hard at something Toby must've just said. From here it's impossible to see her crooked front teeth or the port-wine stain that stretches up from her neck to her jaw. The sun is setting and his hand is on her knee, grazing the hem of her skirt.

I look back at the boy in front of me.

"You don't want to be here," he says.

"What was your first clue?"

"I'm Wes," he says, sticking out his fist to bump.

I ignore this pale, freckled gesture. Instead, I say, "I gotta get home for dinner."

Michaela and Toby are kissing now, still together at the top of the half-pipe. When their faces aren't touching, they are inches apart, smiling, fingers combing through the other's hair. I grab my bike and pedal away without waving goodbye. I pedal hard and fast, trying to rid myself of the moving images of firemen powerwashing concrete, images of his hand on her knee, playing on a loop in my head, until I am dizzy.

When I walk in the front door, wheeling my bike beside me, Dad and Sheila have already gone to bed. All the lights are out, but blue and green and white light is flickering in short bursts from the living room TV set.

I turn the corner and Dave is stretched out on the couch in white boxers and tube socks. His stomach is round, nearly spherical in its beerguttedness, and covered in thick, dark hair. He has a bottle in one hand; the other is down his pants in the masculine way that's supposed to be nonsexual.

I clear my throat to announce my presence, taking a seat in the recliner opposite the couch.

"Hey," he says, without removing his hand, "you missed dinner."

"Dad and Sheila don't usually mind if I'm home too late to eat with them." I shrug.

He sips his beer, eyes trained on the television. "They tell you that, at least."

"Excuse me?"

"They seemed upset," he pauses, taking another swig, "with you, I mean. You should really try to be better."

I snort. "Excuse me?" I say again.

He looks from the television to me. His head is propped up on the armrest, tilted now at an uncomfortable-looking angle. "More respectful," he said. "It wouldn't hurt you to be a good girl."

The hand in his boxers starts to move up and down lightly, pulsating.

I stand to leave, and he offers himself to me through his fly. "Wanna touch it?"

His laughs echo as I run upstairs into my bathroom, to the toilet, where he's left the seat up. Heat is swelling behind my eyes and and bile is swelling up my throat and into view and my phone is vibrating and I know it's Michaela calling to ask where I've gone and why I didn't bother saying goodbye.

Dad and Sheila don't have any baby pictures of me hanging around the house. This is not an affront to me, or anything. It's just that when I was ten, and my parents got divorced, I put stickers over my face in all of them. The stickers were these bright green circles that we used as price tags during the post-divorce garage sale where they sold their wedding china and other relics of their abandoned life together.

Perhaps I thought I fit into that category, because the throughout the sale day I kept trying to cover myself with the little green stickers in hopes that someone might pluck me up from my plastic folding chair and into another life like I was any other thing in our driveway.

My mother wept when she saw what I'd done to the photos, which is the only time I've ever seen her cry. She tried, carefully, to peel them off, but they clung to the photo finish, ripping my face from the photos every time, so I can only assume Mom doesn't have any photos of me hanging either.

Dave asks about this at dinner the next night and I am sure these are the first words he's spoken all day. I tell him about the stickers, silently thankful there are no photos left for him to see or hold or take.

"Oh," he says.

"Yeah," I say, then turn to Sheila and ask to be excused. "May I?" I lift my clean plate an inch or so off the table as evidence.

"You may." She smiles and looks back down at her lap where her work phone sits because she thinks that Dad and I can't see it there.

"I'm staying at Michaela's," I say from the kitchen, over the sound of the water running. They don't answer and I am out the door.

The Getty is the only place in town that won't card me on account of how it's a gas station and not real restaurant or store or anything like that. Michaela and I both know when Sal or Mario will be behind the counter, and they're sure to keep us in tall boys and menthols and anything else we need. Toby, Michaela's Toby, pulls into the Getty's small lot only a minute or so after I walk out.

I lean in his passenger side window. "Where's Michaela?" I ask.

"She'll find us later," he says. "Get in."

His car smells a bit like burnt plastic and it reminds me of Dave. I shake my head. "Everything is wrong," I say.

"How's that?" he asks, already driving, looking ahead.

Instead of answering I pull my feet underneath me on the seat and turn to face Toby. "Let me ask you a question. Which way do you hang a toilet paper roll?"

"What?" He looks away from the road and to me and back to the road again.

"Which way do you hang a toilet paper roll? In or out?"

"What do you mean in or out?"

"Like with the end facing you, or facing the wall?" I showed him using my hands.

"You mean over or under?"

"Yeah, sure."

"Um… Over, I guess."

"So, out?"

He nods.

"Yes!" I exhale loudly and push my feet back to the floor. "Thank you. In is just wrong ."

Toby parks in a cornfield just east of where we go to school and pulls a blanket out of his backseat. We find a spot between two rows of stalks lit by the headlights of his car and set up. The ground is hard and the blanket is thin but we are passing a flask back and forth and we are passing a joint back and forth, and, as we loosen, it matters less and less.

The ground is hard, but Toby is soft, especially his face, or at least it looks that way. His earlobes are gauged and his lip and one eyebrow have rings going through them. I fight the impulse to lean forward and brush my cheek against his, but the urge wins out and I do it anyway. The stubble rakes against my skin.

"What was that?" he asks.

Instead of answering, I sit up straighter. "Did that hurt?" I pull at my lower lip, imitating his piercing.

"Not really," he says. "It's just a pinch." He reaches out and squeezes my lip between his nails.

"Fuck," I say. "That hurt."

"You'll survive."

"Michaela really likes you, Toby," I tell him.

He doesn't answer.

"Do you remember Eskimo kisses?" I ask. "Like this." I lean back over and flutter my eyelashes drunkenly against his cheek, imagining it's Michaela's.

"Those are butterfly kisses, stupid," he says. "Eskimo kisses are like this."

He rubs his nose across my nose, and then again, and then somehow his tongue in my mouth and in almost no time at all he's worked his way inside me.

I'm on my back and there are bits of small stones and other grit working their way into my skin; something sharp and straw-like is cutting into my shoulder. He moves against me and I think about Michaela, how tomorrow we will probably eat grilled cheeses on her couch while I love her and she tells me about how she plans to lose her virginity to Toby, how she thinks she's really in love, and have I ever been in love? And how I will nod and swallow hard and turn away from her, pretending to be very interested in whatever is on TV.

I think about my mother, how she will always be the easiest person to blame for this kind of behavior, how if she were still around she could tell me to make good decisions, and how, if she told me to, I would. I think about Dave and I think about the smell of burning plastic and Toby finishes and I think about how everything is so very, very wrong.

Toby is trying to drive me home and I am trying to let him, but I can't stop shaking.

"Let me out here, okay?" We are at the stoplight between the Taco Bell and the library, a walkable distance from my house.

"Okay."

I slam the door closed and he pulls through the red light.

All the lights in the library are out; its parking lot glows. I cross in front of it and back through the lot to the skate park, fenced in, but unlocked. I swing the gate open and, once inside, try to find the space where I was standing, barefoot, the day before. I look up at the half-pipe, imagining Toby and Michaela the way I had seen them that day, and orient myself accordingly, until I'm sure I have the right spot.

I get down on my knees, and press my face down against the concrete. I want it to be warm, want the ground to show some sign of life, some record of what transpired upon it.

"Everything is wrong," I say. The ground is cold.

I drag my palm gently across the concrete, calming. "Shh…" I say.

I call Wes on my cellphone, the small, freckled boy who told me about the skatepark suicide.

"Hello?" he answers.

"If you could choose how you died, which way would you pick?"

"Um, what?"

I sigh and say instead, "The community pool was drained for the season this morning; I just passed it. Pretty sure it's not covered up yet. We should go."

I sit on the steps in the shallow end watching Wes skate. He is flipping and tricking and I am clapping. I show him my well-practiced back handsprings from cheer season. He applauds my well-practiced back handsprings. He pulls a dented Poland Spring bottle out of his backpack. We do shots of something clear and chemical from the Poland Spring bottle. We race each other from one end of the pool to the other and back again. We take it in turns to lie on our bellies on his skateboard and sled from shallow to deep. We do whip-its from a Reddi-Whip can in the deep end. We spin in circles with our heads back, arms out, mouths open.

We howl at the moon. We curse the light pollution that keeps us from seeing all the non-constellation stars. We lament the absence of their light. We are collapsing into the ground and each other. We are all bruised knees. We are all split lips. We are all dying brain cells. We are laughing, and stomachaches, and stomachs aching from laughter. We are crying. We are terrified of going home. We lie flat in a basin drained of water, pretending to drown. We debate whether it would be worse to drown or to shoot ourselves or to live. We are weighing our options.

On the Road

Hratch Arbach

Meeting with my own ghost that I left there...
in that country,
in that city,
in that house...
in that space...
I used to call it "Home".

A Mother, a Father, a Sister and Brother... Friends, Neighbors...

Do I need to catch that reality? Or reinvent the illusion of a memory,
the memory of space

The journey always starts from your first memory,
somewhere deep inside of you and stays in you, the physical move-
ment of your body is just a vector to guide you to your inner truth.

Whenever you go the journey stays a prisoner of your mind... in your
own space.

We need to feel grounded to something; from a memory to another
we build a history, our history...

Sometimes we even invent memories, bad or good... Who cares?

Hratch... Hratch... Hratch...

We need to have a pass...

Our present, our future, everything happens in yesterday... we live in our yesterdays...

For each memory a ghost is born... we become the space of those ghosts... they haunting us...

They are the traces of our yesterdays; they stay there, holding our memories... waiting for us...

(in Arabic) *"Miyé, Miyé... 7ayala et3a bi Miyé..."*[1]

They come and go, they travel time and space.
They are our heritage, since the genesis! ... the invisible element in our gene...they can be transcripted... divided... cloned...

They are the melody that we whisper suddenly without any reason...

"Sari Aghchig..." (very short traditional Armenian song)

Back to that space

The smell of my Father... His pants are still hanging there...

(in Armenian) *"Hratch... kavatme tchour per, baba..."*[2]

9pm: My Sister laying in here bed, reading " Une Vie " de Maupassant

---

1 " Miyé, Miyé... 7ayala et3a bi Miyé..."
100, 100 ... any piece for 100...
2 " Hratch... kavatme tchour per, baba..."
Hratch... bring me a cup of water, papa...

"On pleure parfois les illusions avec autant de tristesse que les morts "[3]

1am: She's still reading...

My Brother, studying... on his desk lamp is written BEEGEES...
He wants to be a doctor...

                    (in Armenia) *"Hratch... téy me eré hatchis"*[4]

A Mother, still there, her existence belongs to that space...

"Your father he lives with me, he is everywhere..."
"You still here, all of you... can you understand that?"

She finds her way...

To live with ghosts, like a ghost...

in this ghost house...
in this ghost city...
in this ghost country...

                    Alo, Aaaalo... ha Mama... Aalo... Alo...

---

3   "On pleure parfois les illusions avec autant de tristesse que les morts"
We sometimes cry illusions with as much sadness as the dead
4   "Hratch... téy me eré... hatchis"
Hratch... please.. make the tea...

The Girl and the Body

Anya Lewis-Meeks

The girl made dinner pasta with mushrooms and butter, topped with finely grated cheese. Inside the body was quiet, the girl worked happily. She spent many minutes searching for the recipe, carefully assembling the ingredients. *Mise-en-place*. When she grated the cheese, she cut her knuckle, and flakes of her skin fell onto the plate, one single bead of blood. The body whined, but the girl sucked the finger into her mouth, tasting the salty blood and the salty cheese.

The cold butter sizzled as it hit the hot pan. The smell of garlic was sharp and tangy. The roommate came into the kitchen from her room and asked the girl what she was making. The girl told her, and pointed to the bounty of food, the wet, slimy mushrooms, the sizzling melting butter. The cheese scraped into a pile with the tiny flakes of skin.

"Oh my god, don't you think that's so much butter?" The roommate said, her dark eyebrows raised in her pale white face. She rubbed her stomach.

"It's not so much. Just to grease the pan. Also like, it's a treat yourself meal. Obviously. I wouldn't eat it all the time."

"God, but there's so much fat." Shut up, the girl thought. Shut up, don't you wake it.

"Uh, the mushrooms make it kind of healthy."

The roommate smiled, thinly and palely. "I don't like your American mushrooms. They have no flavour. They're just big and full of water. Not like real yummy Taiwanese mushrooms." The roommate left the room. She took her body with her.

The girl tried to return to her cooking. The butter in the pan had gone brown, the chunky milk solids separated from the clear yellowish butterfat. The garlic was blackened and it stuck to the bottom of the pan, improperly lubricated by the butter. The smell in the room was sharp and sour. The girl took the pan from the fire, to pour the brown butter and black garlic into the sink, to start again.

But then the body woke.

The stomach demanded first, a crawling hole of black. The hole pushed outwards into the wall of blood, against the bones, into the skin. Fill me, fill me, fill me. The limbs froze don't you move. I mean it before the hands broke off another knob of butter over the pan, and black garlic unstuck from the bottom of the hot silver pan with the new lubrication. The limbs moved wildly out of the girl's control. They worked the mushrooms in the slimy sauce, they added more and more knobs of butter to the pan. They removed the pasta from the pot, with the tongs but also with the hands, the finger that was scraped on the cheese grater cauterized by the boiling water. The mushrooms leaked their brown juice into the butter and the hand holding the tongs transferred the spaghetti into the wet mixture, stirring, stirring, stirring. All the while the body, the stomach and the limbs and the fingers answering the sucking empty call. The hand tossed the grated cheese into the rich sauce. No sign of the white skin-flakes, the bloody knuckle. The body ate the fuel straight from the skillet, the slurping mouth messy with thick butter. Hot yellow fat splashed on the lips, the cheeks.

"Oh, but it smells so good!" The roommate squealed from her small room. And what will the body do now? How will it explain away the globules of thick hot butter running down its chin, the salty trail left behind as the mouth slurped up the noodle that was stuck there, the tongue licking it into the mouth, the teeth grazing and teasing before biting down.

"Do you want to try some? I was just going to get a bowl." The girl pointed to the cabinet above the kitchen sink. The body let the girl pull the hands up, wipe carefully at the sodden face with a dirty dishrag.

"Nooo, I'll just have a bite." The roommate reached into the skillet with her finger and swirled just one single noodle with her fingertips, she reached deep into the buttery sauce but she emerged with just one noodle. "Mmmmmmm," she moaned.

"You don't want a bowl?"

"Ugh, I can't. I'm way too fat these days." The roommate licked the butter from her spoon, but then she left the kitchen. She returned to her room. She took her small body with her. But the girl had seen it—she had seen the body of the roommate reach out, call towards the food. She had seen the hunger. But the girl had stopped it, hadn't she? She had ignored the body. How? The girl could do it too. She must. She got the cover for the skillet, she put the meal away. She washed up the dishes. Her knuckle stung when she submerged her hand in the soapy dishwater, but not enough to wake the sleeping body.

And later, when the roommate slept, in her small room with her small obedient body, the girl's unruly body emerged again. It took her to the skillet, with the tongs in its unfrozen limbs and it forced the food into its mouth, it slurped the spaghetti and its teeth squeaked against the brown mushrooms and the food filled its stomach, pushing out and out and out. Until the skillet was empty, its tongue licking the skillet clean and silver. The girl, quiet and shameful. The body awake, still, and wanting.

Morning, Motherfucker

Jason Koo

Just popped the collar of my robe in this motherfucker,
I.e. kitchen, as I make some sweet-ass hash browns.
Is that the start of a poem? It's barely the start of breakfast.
Noon light comes streaming through the window.
Is that the start of a poem? My landlady—what a word—
Just told me to be out of here by July 1. At first I wrote
Just told me to be out of her. Slightly different poem.
The millionaires buying her brownstone, milling past me
As I cranked this up in my robe at this motherfucker,
I.e. dining table, wondering if it could indeed be a poem,
Demand it. I'm gonna squat right here in this kitchen,
I.e. motherfucker, with my million-dollar syntax and hash browns
And make those motherfuckers mill around me for life.
I'll miss this motherfucking beautiful neighborhood
Of Whitman & Auden & Crane & Mailer & McCullers
& Miller & Miller & Smith & Wolfe & motherfucker
How many more writers could live in these brownstones?
How many more ampersands could live in contemporary poetry?
Now there are probably no writers here except me.
Oh, and little known former Poet Laureate of America
Phil Levine on Willow St. And fellow Asian American male poet
Ken Chen, also on Willow St. I wonder if they too pop the collars
Of their robes as they make some sweet-ass hash browns.
Mailer surely popped the collar of his robe. He probably
Put on boxing gloves to take his hash browns out of the oven.

Hart Crane I can't see ever making, let alone eating, hash browns.
Just too much cranium to contain in one kitchen.
Whitman couldn't have eaten just one hash brown, or two,
He had to be making whole schools of hash browns,
40,000 hash browns forked with 40,000 motherforking forks.
He would've written about all the potato fields they came from,
Sunsets over the cool brown earth that made their beds.
Henry Miller likely would've fucked his hash browns.
Auden would've had his hash browns at an appropriate time
Scheduled into the morning. Last night I talked about
That motherfucker's face. What a motherfucking poet's face.
Was Auden ever young? Did he come out of his mother's vagina
Already wrinkled? Imagine that vagina. Auden's face
Like a hash brown out of that vagina. I'm feeling better,
In spring, in this motherfucking beautiful light. I'm dancing
In this motherfucker, i.e. kitchen, as I flip these hash browns
And think I can start to begin to forget you some day.

Best American Citizen

Citizen is a great book, the first great book
I've read in a while, a while that is so funny

but not so funny, in which I was doing
a lot of things that piled up into nothing,

like the loose change you insert into a box
then forget about. Meanwhile Rankine

was sitting in this book waiting for me
to be opened, because when you open

a great book it is really you that is opened.
I liked that thought a moment ago but now

enh. Consciousness, how to capture this
funny-not-so-funny while, Rankine does it

well in this book—I almost wrote "a great job"
but remembered how I told my students

to stop signing off critiques "Great job!"
especially after they've just pointed out

a poem's flaws. I didn't really understand
this poem, you should fix all your grammar

and use more concrete imagery like Professor
said. Great job! Consciousness is one thing

I left out of my holy trinity of threshold
poetry requirements, though I think it is there

in the voice/tone/drama. You are imprinting
your consciousness onto the page, you are

becoming an utterance. I like what Rankine
does with the you of her book, how she makes

the drama of being—beginning—a you
emerge. You are you even before you

grow into understanding you
are not anyone, worthless,

not worth you. Just expertly enjambed.
All the white critics weighing in on the back

of the book, including one of the great
institutional racists of our time, ironically

praising the exposure of exactly the kind
of racism she practices: "a racism so guarded

and carefully masked as to make it all the more
insidious…" I wonder how Rankine felt

about that. Maybe they are friends.
Maybe the poet couldn't pass up the honor

of the Great White Badge, as already I am seeing
young poets of color post on Facebook news

of their inclusion in the new *Best American Poetry*,
as if that little yellowface incident last year

never happened, as if they didn't act enraged
like everyone else, so happy are they to be included,

finally, that they won't show solidarity
with their POC peers. And what if I got the call

I've never gotten? So much bitterness built up
I'd probably—probably—reject it, though

I'd have to make a show of this rejection
on Facebook or other social media, and there

you have it, the institution wins again.
My CV is now over twelve pages long, absurd,

just yesterday I was putting a couple of things in
I forgot to include for my institutional review

and still, somehow, I don't exist, not really.
You only begin to exist for the Great White Badge

when you complain of the bitterness of being
unable to begin. I wonder how long Rankine

felt this way, probably still feels this way,
especially after losing the National Book Award

to Louise Glück, whom I see, interestingly,
she thanks on her acknowledgements page.

Greg Pardlo wins the Pulitzer and they ask
the Great White Badge what he thinks of this,

he hems and haws about how to describe
Pardlo's poetry as if he's read it, which he has

not, what he means to say is, I have no idea
how this guy won except because he's black.

Vijay Seshadri wins the year before and people
think, Oh I get it, the first Asian American winner

in poetry. I still haven't read Vijay's new book,
and only bought it after he won the Pulitzer.

I was as surprised as anyone else, and surprised
when Pardlo won, and of course I too had

the thought Did he just win because he's…?
but also thought, Well shit if Vijay can win it,

so can I, if Pardlo can win it, so can I,
these guys had hardly won *anything* before,

no one read them, just a few months before
Vijay won I saw him at a Cave Canem party

and asked him how his book was doing
and he said he *thought* it was doing well, one

never really knows with these things, i.e.
it was doing nothing, and then, lo, it wins

the Pulitzer. And suddenly it matters for all
the people who ignored the book before,

suddenly they have opinions on this poet
though they're thinking, He only won it because

he's…and my thought is You're goddam right
he won it *because he's*, why shouldn't he?

All those years before he didn't matter
because he's…and now he gets to begin

that sentence a different way. Is it better
when someone wins because they're white?

Louise Glück won and I thought, Well she
just won because she's white. If Rankine

had won people would've thought, Well she
just won because she's black. Anyone can

easily see that we are moving in a circle.
Who cares about awards, yeah, but the awards

are what get you *read*. You have to be out there
so much people have no choice but to read

you, eventually your name, your book,
get lodged in their consciousness even if

they don't want them there. I might
never have read *Citizen* had it not gotten

the press it did, had it not been nominated
for the National Book Award, though

at some point all that press started making me
not want to read it because it seemed like

the book we were to read on race, according
to the Great White Badge. You see how much

threatens the reading of a single great book,
how little chance it has of actually happening.

How many poets have I invited to read
for my series or talked to who have never

read my books? Never even heard of them?
I'm sure some of them probably want to

or intend to read one at some point, they
might have even read a poem or two online.

It takes years, for whatever reason, to sit
down and read a book. A book has to be read

on its own time. So many books I've read
and they're sitting stacked all around me,

but when it comes time to make a syllabus
I don't know which ones *really* matter to me.

Or, well, I do, but they also have to be books
I think will matter to my students and that

I haven't read in a while, so they'll be fresh.
And so *The Trial* and *Blindness* along with *Citizen*.

But next semester the books will probably
be different. Probably. I have used probably

many times this morning. Probably I am
unsure of a lot of what I have said. Probably.

River

Jessica Denzer

1. The Memory: Yes, the sky was beautiful today. Yes the sky was beautiful today. Tomorrow it will rain, and the rain will carry the dirt to the water. And the words will slip out of my mouth and fall through my fingers, crawl to the ground, etch shapes in the mud.

2. In 1803, Napoleon sold the Louisiana Territory of New France to the United States for fifty million francs. Fifty million francs is less than three cents per acre, the cheapest land deal the US has ever made. The shape of the land, when drawn on a map, resembles a heart, the bottom ventricle bleeding into the Gulf of Mexico. An 828,000 square mile organ. The heartland. Later, this territory will be renamed the Missouri Territory and gain the Red River Valley south of the 39th parallel. Later still, the state of Missouri will join the Union as the 24th state—breaking up the territory, fracturing the whole, splintering the heart, renaming the land.

3. Missouri: etymology, origin: not the French word for misery. French word for misery: misère. To be filled with suffering, à être rempli de tristesse extrême. To experience extreme poverty, or to be excluded from society. Pour découvrir l'extrême pauvreté, ou d'être exclus de la société. Missouri: a word adapted by French colonists from the Miami-Illinois language of the Algonquian—Niúachi, *not French*, People full of water, fruitful, filled, without want. People of the River Mouth.

4. My mother swings us on the porch swing, singing "Red River Valley". The second story porch has a nicer view. Even later, after years of neglect, of forgetfulness, of rain and wind and stray cats, there will be the most amazing light moving in and out of the mesh screen that holds us in. The light is purple and blue and pink and yellow, reflecting off the deep colors of the Evergreens:

From this valley they say that you are leaving.
We will miss your bright eyes and sweet smile.
For they say you are taking the sunshine
That has brightened our path for a while.

Eventually, the porch swing will break. We will leave it unfixed and dangling from a single chain. One summer, the thunderstorms will tear through the mesh screens and throw the swing in multiple directions until it finally falls flat on the floor, making a crash that will wake us all up in the middle of the night. The morning after the storm, I will peek through the windows to see it sitting there, alone, like something amputated, disabled and abandoned. This is the year the cats inherit the porch.

5. River: etymology: from Latin rīpa, "bank", rīpārius, "riverbank", rīpāria, "land by the water's edge", not the water, itself. Place where the water stops. Where it is subtracted, where is flows to an end, where it closes its mouth. Missouri River: people full of water's end. People of the River Mouth. The river winds its muddy waters around your waist, carrying you from place to place. Little baby Moses, floating in his tiny canoe, on the back of the Lehemi Bird Woman, the Snake Woman, the Boat Puller, a name we never learned to pronounce, trading her voice for a face on the dollar coin. Little baby, she will name you Jean Baptiste because you are the water prophet, and she will show the strange men the skin of the land, its curvatures

and bones. They write it in a book, call it surveying, stake their claim. In the mud banks there are cracks, a map, marking the buying, and selling, and taking of land.

6. In 1858, a poor daughter of a miller and a laundress was gathering firewood in a limestone cave-grotto of Massabielle, a cluster of rocks bordered by the Gave de Pau river. There, at a spring in the grotto, she was struck with a vision of a young lady in white and blue. Bernadette, fourteen and on her knees, the limestone digging into her skin, bruising and scraping against her bones and muscle, she listened to the lady—The Immaculate Conception, The Virgin Mother, Mary Mother of God—*Build me a church here, where the stone feeds the water. Here on this rock, build me a church.*

7. My father calls me from France. It's his first time traveling across the Atlantic. He is in Lourdes on a Catholic pilgrimage he agreed to go on with his uncle. They have traveled to the healing waters of Our Lady of Lourdes, where Bernadette saw her vision. Here, as a member of the Knights of Malta, my great uncle hopes to heal his shingles.

I'm at work, but I pick up anyway.

"Dad," I say, "Aren't you in France?"

"Yes, Jay, and I'm sitting here on the balcony of my hotel, looking out across the French countryside, the sun setting over the horizon. I can see an ancient castle that was once conquered by Charlemagne."

"Wow," I say, but am angry because I cannot listen because I am at work and have to worry about the less important needs of less important people. I cannot hear the story being told by my father.

"I wanted to call you tonight because earlier there was a festival," he continues, "and there was a band playing traditional French folk songs. I hadn't ever heard any of them, of course. But I listened, and after a while I realized I recognized a song. It was "Red River Valley". They were singing it in French, but I knew all the words, and it made me so happy because I could hear your mother singing it to you girls, and you girls singing it back to your mother, and all three of you singing at once. Remember the porch swing? She used to sit you girls on that swing and the whole neighborhood would listen."

8. I remember all the words. I can sing them to you right now. There are hundreds of stories pulling from the root of that song. Rolling off my breath, tumbling out of my mouth, flowing to the floor.

9. Like the Missouri River, the Red River was a major trade route, contributing to the settlement of North America. The river forms the border between Minnesota and North Dakota, the valley floor spreading out like a quilt west and north and south. The river's tributaries follow the valley like thin arms on a map, like pulsating veins pushing water out from the center towards the Missouri River, calling out: *Sister, I'm here.*

10. Fort Orleans, the first European fort on the Missouri River, was established in 1723 by French explorer Étienne de Veniard, Sieur de Bourgmont. Originally stationed at Fort Pontchartrain, what is now Detroit, Étienne was caught in the middle of a war between the Ottawa and the Miami Indians. Firing recklessly from their position, he and his men shot a French priest and then deserted their posts. Near Pontchartain, he met the daughter of the chief of the Niúachi tribe and accompanied her to the Niúachi village at the mouth of the Missouri. *La Grande Riviére*, he whispered in his dreams, *on this water I will build my fort.* There, he married the Niúachi princess, who bore him several children, including a son named le Petit Missouria.

11. As a child, I think I can starve myself for God. I think I can stay up all night in devotion. I never do. I eat. I fall asleep. But I envision myself on my knees, my hands hard pressed together, my little body

covered in light. I listen for a voice calling me, asking me for my bruises. Bernadette was fourteen when the Virgin came to her in the limestone caves. Missouri is filled with limestone, and I am younger than fourteen, so why not me? I convince my parents to take me to the emergency room twice, complaining of stomach pains. One cannot be holy and fully healthy.

During Mass, I try to kneel the longest. The other kids allow their thighs to rest against the wood of the pew, but not me. I tighten my muscles until they burn, pressing my knees harder into the thin vinyl cushion of the kneeler, my elbows propped against the rail, my knuckles red and white and clasped together. If I could, I would kneel on the pink marble floor because the pain would make me closer to God. On Sundays, when I serve as an acolyte, dressed in white robes, I relish holding the large red Bible for the priest to read from. The gold letters gleam down at me from under the shadow of his body, reciting over and over, blood and body, blood and body.

At home, I have a picture Bible, small and yellow, full of realistic illustrations designed to look like oil paintings. There is one particular image I obsess over. I memorize it. Jesus tempted in the desert. But it's not Jesus I am interested in. It is the other figure standing over him. Muscular, red, winged, ugly: Satan promising kingdoms. How can something so terrible have kingdoms to hand out?

I have nightmares. This red-winged angel coming to me, holding out his hand. I hear my own voice, a voice in my head, "Yes, I will give you everything." The "yes" is immediately followed up with a "No! I was just kidding. Sorry!" But the yes was thrilling to give. Yes! Yes! I am afraid of myself.

I know I will never be holy.

12. In 1725, de Bourgmont returned to France with several Indian Chiefs. The plan was to show the delights of Paris: the opera, hunting, and touring the palaces. His Niúachi bride was brought along,

listed as a servant. The tribesmen returned that year, along with the Niúachi bride but de Bourgmont stayed behind. He already had a wife in France. *On this rock*, whispers St. Peter, *I will build my church; I will write my story, but only after the cock crows three times, only after I have denied and abandoned my love.* Niúachi, daughter of the leader, body used and abandoned, you gave your greatest gift. You are the People of the River Mouth, Le Grande Riviére, Missouri River, Muddy River, it flows from Étienne, to France, to Jean Baptiste. John the Baptist at the river mouth, what should we testify?

13. Do you think Napoleon ever thought of Missouri? Of the land he gave away? The heart of it all. Alone on St. Helena, did he ever think of the muddy banks of the river?

14. The Memory: Recently, I had a dream. Napoleon and I are in a house. Outside is the river. Napoleon stands behind me, a young Corsican. His hair is a little long, his curls brushing tenderly over his forehead. I have my back to him but somehow I can still see his face, a scowl across his small pink lips, his blue eyes. When he was a boy, he constantly found himself in the shadow of his older brother, but it was the youngest brother he loved, and the youngest brother who died. How many stories must we read with this formula? Always in the shadow of the older boy, the one who was destined for greatness before you were even born, whose mythology forces you to rise up angrily and take and take and take until there is nothing more to take? We are told that Napoleon's brother was a grand disappointment, a great passionate failure. He should have been Emperor.

In my dream the river floods and the water flows around the house, and all the windows are open. As the water begins to rise, a horse slips in through a window. And then the water pours into the house. The water is crystal blue and beautiful. I crawl onto a pile of rocks and see the Boat Puller, Bird Woman, Charon, Styx, I see the women of the river on the other side, I see them, and I see all the words, all the words falling into the water.

M TRAIN

Nicodemus Nicoludis

I am no longer fortitudinous.
Or even adequately plucky.
I can still stay out late but mostly
wake up early now
& think of mountains somewhere else
where walking is gliding.
But mostly, I think I'd drive,
which is romantic & sort of sexy.
The road getting blacker
& blacker
each mile further from home.
Or closer to work
I would imagine.

Something about time as movement
you control. Then I hear
that metal tube
coursing through Queens
suddenly. Heavy metallic
the nausea of the morning
& my dreams of being very
very small
still cloudy & elusive
filled with other people
maybe braver, or at least
more blasé about
what it means to be stuck,
inhibited by your brain
or other chemicals
faking being feelings,
resilient to forget July 2nd.

I like to look down
& to know that
the ground is just there.
Examine every part & see
how each runs,
pauses.

Ha, the sky.
Ha, these clouds.

Seeming legendary
in their brief & hollow fly-bys.

Here are my supernova hands,

        my little burning

    stars of anxiety,

       my ash

          multiplying

             from forest fires

across most of the Western

                 US & Canada

hands.

      Needles & pins,

          needles & pins

   like

      Jackie DeShannon (1963)
      The Searchers (1964)
      Smokie (1977)
      The Ramones (1978)
      Tom Petty and The Heartbreakers w/ Stevie
      Nicks live (1985).

Feet sing,
& all at once
want to give out
as I stare
across the car:
the middle-aged man
so skinny
*well how can he help
me if he wanted to?*

I hear it crash
along the rails
they fix perennially
& think about
what if?

A simple construction.

My eyes & heart
stuck here, trapped
in the part of the past
they only know how to

adequately—   no
appropriat—   no
reflexively react to
from prior traumatic experience.

The memory of
body & mind
& their connection
broke for a little while—

            a ripple in a pond
with no water but clear,
            no pebbles tossed,
but little saplings
            of electricity.

Little funny sparks
            in grey flesh

bend & bend.

Maybe it takes
only a little bit of prayer,
breath control,
forgiving yourself
for your life,
the lives of others
you want
from the outside,
shortcomings & regrets.
& life,
our love, like
an open-pit mine
expanding outward
into the pristine,
now-dying countryside,
can never get filled
with enough rain
to make it level again.

Often it's admitting
that we live
in a deeply sick society.

What is to be done?
We still don't have an answer.

I'm sorry Vladimir, Leon, Rosa, Salvador, &c.

So, I walk this morning

to get some pills.

My little pills.

My forgetting brain,

give it the life
it had once,
where I used to look across

the East River
from the Q or M train.

Hmm that was nice once.

I write a sketch,
   this poem,
at my desk
   this morning
thinking of you
   still in bed
hoping that
   now this
really is courage.

A little bit of luck
   & we both know
how to get something
     closer to well
together. But
   at least we
have a home
   together to
process
   fear in the abstract—

its usual form.

Little by little
   each time
I hear the train
   cursing through
our window
   I think

Ya well, fuck you too.

From Gas Stations at Night (Wild Radio 1) by Brent Kite & Chris Molnar (2015)

From Gas Stations at Night (Wild Radio 1) by Brent Kite & Chris Molnar (2015)

From Artifacts of the Moon (Wild Radio 2) by Brent Kite & Chris Molnar (2017)

From On the Road by Hratch Arbach (2019) (top) / From Top 40 (Wild Radio 3) by Brent Kite & Chris Molnar (2019) (bottom)

I Was Going To Tell You Something And Then I Forgot What It Was

Joanna C. Valente

You almost cry when your boss
pants in frustration when you can't
hear her. It's not like you want
to be deaf, you almost tell her. It's not like
you want to feel as though your life
is falling apart. When she asks you to report
on a divorce study, you do. Ignore the irony,
ignore the ache in the back of your throat
like an ostrich squeezing out of your mouth
when she makes the joke, divorce is contagious.
Maybe you should find better friends.
When you ask your other
boss for a raise and she tells you no
and you forget why you asked in the first
place when you knew she would say no
and everyone is making more than you
and you know it's personal, you're
replaceable. You make them uncomfortable
in your difference. You aren't like them.
They don't like that. They don't like difference.
They don't care about bodies without binaries.
It makes them feel threatened. But no one actually
admits that. Your union rep is appalled
by what you tell her and you remember the first time

you cried at a job. You were 16 and a man
insisted you put the wrong code for peaches
into the supermarket's register. Your manager
came over, said you were right. He left
angry. There's that other time you cried
at a job when you were called useless.
They were right.

On Mobile Slaughterhouses

Evan Gorzeman

In 2010 a mobile slaughterhouse facility received USDA approval, known by the mechanically stiff name: Modular Harvest System, or the MHS, for short. The unit consists of three green Lego brick family vacation-style trailers. The MHS can be moved from ranch to ranch, farm to farm, processing large animals down to grocery-store-sized, customer ready, hunks of meat. Farmers now do not need to worry about transporting large amounts of animals to a traditional abattoir. Everything is stress free and on the go.

The three trailers are so: the first trailer the cows or goats or llamas or what have you are calmly led up the ramp where they are stunned and killed. The next trailer processes the animal down to conventional cuts of meat and they are stored in a cold environment so as not to spoil. The last trailer is for nonsummable parts, this is the offal and the manure and the dregs which are processed into no-edible items ready for different consumes. Again, this process is stress free and the MHS can be packed up and be back on the road again in under three hours.

The entire process has led me to try my hand at imagist poetry. Here's an attempt:

> Now this cow is dead
> We have killed it
> Hang the hoofs to the rafters
> Blood from rusty spigot

Modern day slaughterhouses are designed to be calm places. The most interesting aspect of the design is the ramp that leads each animal closer to the stunning bolt. It's the curve of the ramp that soothes the doomed bovine. Think of parking garages. Think the Guggenheim Museum, think of how calm both of these places are. Think of the cows last walk around the bend. Think of problems that don't need solving and solve them. We can taste the stress in the burger. Think of your stressed-out bodied consuming another stressed-out body. We can all agree it's better to be stress free.

Here is another poem:

Freeze-dried meat
Vacuum sealed for freshness
Thoughts and feelings
On sale next week

Do not pity this cow, do not pity the plush leather interior of a Mercedes C Class, for it died, calmly, years ago. Do not YouTube the process of leather tanning. Do not write think pieces on Mobile Slaughterhouses with pun-filled titles butchering classic literary works such as "A Movable Beast".

I have been to a slaughterhouse. Years ago, before a butcher on wheels was FDA approved. There was blood flowing out of the old wood paneling and empty cow hides stretched out on racks to dry in the sun. This is what my family did when they emigrated to America because it was what their family did back home. Maybe they thought it would be something I would do. It was also something I should not have seen, having snuck away from my parents. The process was violent, even in the haze of early childhood memory I can see the weight and strain of the animal hitting the floor, and the rattle of life leaving the cow's body.

Days after the cows are gone you can hear the corn grow. You may think it is some person far off in the fields, shucking an ear to eat for themselves. But in the stillness, you can hear the corn itself sprout, listen for yourself the next time you stand alone, calmly, and there is no one there.

Defending Oneself

Caitlin Forst

#1

Jackie knows better than to tell the men in the online chatroom that her driveway winds through the forest for five miles, that the cabinet under her kitchen sink is crowded with her mom's Maker's Mark bottles, that her older brother paints deer vertebrae and sells them out on the highway from a stand like apples.

She is honest with the men, though, about being a 14 year old girl. Teaching herself to refract, to be all girls in all fantasies, hypothetical and real.

#2

Jackie turns 17 the same week her first boyfriend turns 28.
She watches him rope a horse's neck to a rod in the stable of his step-dad's farm.
He's sweating when she asks him, "What's your thing?"
He tells her that he doesn't have one.
"Everyone has a thing," she says.
He admits only to PornHub videos featuring girls with eyes the same color as hers.
She tries to think of an excuse to go home, but now he wants to know.
He presses her with bad guesses that are all so boring they offend her.
After a half hour of this, she tells him, "I like to be degraded."

#3

Jackie sleeps in her manager's apartment most nights, although she never pays him rent.

She is the one to split a six pack with the landlord when her wife leaves her for one of the other tenants.

There's a permanent stain on the bedroom carpet from the time she drunk ate a pomegranate.

A plumber answers her call when the shower drain gets clogged with her hair.

Still, ten days before they're meant to move to California together, he lifts the bottom drawer of his dresser and throws the whole if it in the backseat of her trunk.

"We lived together at least long enough to both gain weight and stop having sex!" she yells at his retreating back.

There were just a few articles of her clothing in that drawer and nothing else.

#4

Jackie rents a place in North Hollywood with a hundred year old ceiling that El Nino will, months later, break open. A man barks like a dog in the alley outside. She climbs the fire escape to her roof alone, and looking at the glowing Hilton hotel sign aimed towards her face she sends a text: "Do you think the anticipation of pain is always worse than the pain itself?" But the message stalls forever without the proper cell service to send.

#5

Jackie and her fiancé drive past a shirtless man in downtown Los Angeles wrapping a plastic bag around a streetlamp. The man is smiling, susceptible to no one.

Without prompting, she tells Kyle for the third time that she does not feel nervous to be naked in public.

He lives up to his promise to never inhibit her impulses. There's a silence and she offers him a variation in an even tone as they pull up to the gallery: "Other men are going to see my nipples tonight." He grabs the back of her neck with one hand without moving his eyes from the road.

As she undresses in the yoga studio under the pretense of liberating her body from the context of sexualization, she thinks of Kyle's mom cornering her in a restaurant the day before. She was weeping in desperation then, trying to convince her God was real. Now, Jackie's certain she'll bring whatever she loves down to hell with her, including him.

Satan Says, *I'll Get You Out*

Mina Hamedi

1.

A one-armed woman serviced a man behind the taco shack. The man said his family was from Georgia, the country.

The bartender said he was letting his hair grow long again and he bailed his co-worker from jail a few nights ago.

The musician lived in his dreams. He wanted to stay asleep longer, to feel what could be, not what is.

I don't dream that way. I play out a scene in my mind and hope it'll follow me when I close my eyes. Sometimes it works, sometimes it doesn't.

2.

The girl remembered the friend who died nine years ago. Today is the day, she said. No one responded.

The friend told her that he'd loved her when they were kids. Oh, what could've been, she wondered.

The mother left her husband and moved to Florida with her boyfriend from high school. She took the cats with her.

The husband wouldn't listen. You don't hear things when they are said by the people who love you. You need strangers to prove you need help.

I've asked for help many times this year. But I'm learning how to stop helping.

3.
The director loved gore and desperation. She was going on a camping trip soon but promised to reach out when she returned.

The daughter wondered how her mother made her. She tore apart her insides, wrapped herself in viscera. She made certain she'd be the last one to grow in that body.

The agent paced up and down the halls of the office. His breath smelled like coffee and his words needed reassurance.

The boy wanted to feel things. I want to feel things, too. I will never be done feeling. I hate, and I love.

4.
The man looked at her every morning when he made her coffee. His green eyes, the only bright thing in that darkened corner behind all the filters, and taps, and steam.

The boss was frantic, unpredictable. But she said the same thing when she had to get off the phone: *Alright, my darling.*

The student said it's a miracle that we are all walking; that we are alive. He's torn ligaments in his hands many times. Once, when he woke up from surgery, he told his wife he had over three hundred peanut butter sandwiches that year.

I can't stop things from going wrong. There are times when I feel like I can survive anything. But I'm tired now.

5.

The writer has a skull on his desk. He holds it when he gets stuck. He grabs a notebook, writes a title on each page and fills it up.

The driver walks by her desk every other day with just a smile and a hand raised for a five. He asks how things are going and in the middle of even the worst moments, she raises her hand too.

The uncle cries. My father created a miracle for us, he says. We have to keep it alive. The nieces and nephews surround him.

The cousin moves closer to her face, I don't want to hurt you, please step back. He takes off, down the pier and to the ocean.

That is the only violence I'll witness, until I cause it.

6.

The follower sat in the red chair by the window. She closed her eyes and moved her fingers slowly over the string of beads. Her lips were moving at first but then everything was still.

The son lifted the white cloth from her mother's face. He looked, then covered it back up again. He climbed out of the grave and threw a handful of soil.

The assistant willed the tears away as people rounded the corner to her desk. She typed someone else's words.

The editor fell during a stressful week. She recently had to remove the stitches from her face. She kept apologizing for taking up time, taking up space.

My scalp itches and I bleed because thoughts become physical. Because you think and your body feels it. Don't tell me this is not how it happens.

7.
The father sent well wishes at the beginning of each week. He worried over numbers, loved ones, countries. He started riding horses again. A delicate balance of control.

The grandfather tried to hold on but he couldn't. Blood marked the carpeted floor; a trail for the police to stare at as they questioned his wife. A mother was once questioned, too. The cat had dropped a glass plate on the daughter's head and everyone was suspicious.

The niece held the baby in her arms, her elbow supported by a pillow. Here is a being we have not ruined yet, she thought. Maybe someday, she can make her own.

The lawyer ran up and down the halls in panic. He brought people to his office and told them exactly what he was thinking, what he was planning. He got up to leave, opening doors but closing them a few more times before truly leaving. A few more secrets. Tactics.

I always find out, anyway.

8.
The doctor tilted her head. She gently pushed the patient's hair away. Then, she checked the joints, listening to the bones. The elbows, knees, fingers, sacrum. By now, she could see beneath the skin. The

architect led her team. She stood on site and imagined what she could build. She sailed, ropes cutting through skin. She took care of a beast that never listened to her.

The gardener tried to save the stray animals but there were too many. They were all sick. Limp, infected jaws, parasites in their brains— suspending motor functions. So many buried in beautiful gardens lines with jasmine and roses.

The artist was the last of his kind. Trances followed by extreme discipline. Notebooks filled with ideas and images. Paint-covered shoes. A muse in the form of a beautiful woman, nicknamed, "Panther."

To have such a strong purpose. What is that like?

9.
The guide shared ancient stories as he placed his hand over limestone walls and marked where the sands and waters receded. He believed all the stories came from one source.

The girlfriend took long walks, sometimes two-three hours twice in one day. She watched children race off in front of parents, the crazed muttering under their breath. That line is so thin, the girlfriend thought, between what is real and what isn't.

The astrologer said past lives are real. This is not the only you that ever was. You were your mother's mother. You were burned for your words. You knew him, before all of this. You knew but you forgot.

The grandmother has a death book. She writes the dates and names of friends and family members who have died, including the particular circumstances of their deaths. When the notebook fills up, she begins a new one.

The singer sang about salvation. When she reached the high, painful notes, she'd push her platinum hair back and make herself larger. *I got demons and they're wrestling*, she roars.

So many demons.

10.
Remember that eclipse two summers ago? It was around this time.

The world shifted that afternoon.

We gathered above New York on balconies and roofs and looked at the sun through filters, waiting to feel differently.

I did feel differently. How can you not believe these things will change you? Change your blood, the fire in your brain, or the way you breathe?

I feel like people are the same way. They change you.

Worlds offered to you.

What do you do?

Erwartung

Jameson Fitzpatrick

worse than being stood up by a stranger
your lover is late
could be anywhere
could be with her

is not with you
all the available information
is little comfort
should have worn a jacket

Chorus

If you must go involving yourself
in the night's business,

be discreet!

lest you wake devotion,
light-sleeping.

Once you've seen its face you see it forever,
and nothing else!

Expectation

I stood in the forest a long time,
a lady in waiting. The night

grew longer and longer until
finally something brushed my shoulders

—not him, but my own hair
reaching down.

Summer

It was once
I remember

how green and light

Sometimes it rained
you were faster

out of the trees
back up the hill

Possible Body

I could have sworn
it was the smooth brown trunk of him

I found wet and lifeless before me.

Just a trick of the
absence of light. Fallen tree.

no answer no matter
how many times you call

out his name
over and over

oh, what a little moonlight can do
oh, what a little moonlight can do to you

lunacy from the Old French
lunatique meaning insane

from the Latin lunaticus
meaning moonstruck

Chorus

How cold you must have been, poor
girlie boy. You were a crying blonde voice
we couldn't shut up.

: In Here?
: Is This The Way Yet?
: Do You See Back There
: So Strange But Is Your Eye
: Come As A Light!
: He Is Also Not As
: The Moonlight
: There Is No Place For Me
: Dearest, Dearest, The Morning Comes

End of the Chase

When exhausted
the hunter still might have caught the fox

but no longer cared to;
all he loved of it then was its running.

Chalkboard

Nifath Karim Chowdhury

How do you _____? Do you stuff a fist into your mouth, biting on your knuckles, choking on your tongue, feeling the back of your throat stinging from not being able to _____ loud enough? Do you sit on the subway, squashed by strangers, cushioned by the sounds of their voices from all sides and _____ with your lips pursed, like a kettle getting ready to whistle, a pressure cooker about to burst, daring yourself to go a decibel higher, daring anyone to notice. Do you _____ with a bottle at your lips, a stranger between your legs, thoughts of a bleak tomorrow swirling in your head. Do you _____ a little every time you laugh, every time you lie. Do you like the corner, the dark corner, the lonely corner, where you can put your hands up against the wall, bury your nose in it, and _____, pretending like you can't be seen. Do you know the sound of your father's footsteps, the slow drag of his feet in sandals at home, the smart snap of his heel against pavement on his way to work? Do you _____when you think of that sound ceasing? Do you have a headache? Do you want to rub your temples, index and middle finger going in small circles against your skull, digging until they break through, touching brain. Do you know how to breathe? Can you teach me? Do you _____ in your sleep? I don't know, I've never slept with you. Do you know how to make chicken soup without it tasting like a fever? Do you _____ every time you do it wrong? Do you want to rip your hair out, one by one, or by the bunches, holding them in your hand like a bouquet of frayed, bloody stems? Do you _____ when you think of home, of being "too late", of all the ways in which light can turn to dark? Do you _____ when you do math? Do you have pillows for two people on your bed? Will you need them? Do you wear heels because they hurt? Do you _____ at the touch of every new lover, every new hand that feels wrong on your skin? Do you dream the same dreams that I do? Do you feel the world in colour like I do? Why do you make yourself so difficult to love?

Draft Dodgers (Excerpt)

Etan Nechin

A barge on the Ohio River: it does not move like a boat, does not rock and bobble upon the eddies. It sails upstream, silently, a stagnant mass of metal on silk water, pushed by a rusty tugboat. If it were detached, the barge would get swept downstream and slip into the Mississippi River, until it would finally spill into the Gulf of Mexico. My father, at twenty-four, is standing on one of those barges, somewhere between Kentucky and Illinois. The river: the word originally meant the river bank, where the water ends, the limits of the land. How can you name what is constantly moving, changing, speak of it as anything but unchartable, unknowable in its magnitude and depth, to dare to know where that absence of river would lead? The Ohio River, with its murky water claimed so many lives, so many stories. My father is wearing a new pair of rubber boots. The guy who hired him to work on the barge, to strap containers onto the metal platform, a friend of my grandfather's, upon looking at the bell-bottomed, big-bearded beatnik, shook his head and said, Boy, before you start, you better get rid of those cowboy boots, 'less you wanna slip and break your goddang neck. From where my father is standing, leaning on the metal rig, it feels like the barge is still, that it's a river bank. It's only that, if he would have tried to step off, he'd realize he was standing on an island.

The moment I am born into consciousness: I am three years old, perhaps. I am standing on the porch of our half-built house. My mom is not there. She might've been talking to the contractor, a friend of my parents who helped my father build the house. The house is made from stone and concrete. In Israel, it seems that all houses are made with concrete. Perhaps, after years of displacement, people are trying to create a sense of permanence, or maybe they are already building shelters to protect them from the inevitable devastation. My parents' house, our house, which houses this first memory, was planned by an architect, another friend of my father who lived in the village. His design for the house was based on a bunch of used windows my father found in the flea market down in the Turkish Market—windows with chipped frames surrounded by stone and concrete. In my memory, I am on the porch, waiting for my father to arrive. In my memory, I can hear the engine struggling down the limestone path. My father steps out of the car. I run to him, but I miss a step and fall, my head knocking against the just-dried concrete. In my memory, I don't hear myself crying. All I remember is my father picking me up. The blood from my forehead drips on his green uniform, drips on the path. My mother takes me and rinses my face with the hose. The bleeding stops, but the blood seeps into the uniform, creating a stain that turns the khaki dark green. The bloodstain spreads, it sustains.

It was in the Presidio, perhaps, that my father first thought of light. They wanted to bury him with inventory lists, hide him in a martial maze of bureaucracy. At twenty-three, my father was sitting behind the desk at the supply unit store, reading Tolstoy, in Russian, for the last time; he had been on forced hiatus from his studies. The army insisted, until his case reached a resolution. Besides, his interest didn't lie in literature that told of a bygone era, in the language of his grandparents anymore—the language he was sent to study, now the language of the enemy. He was reading pamphlets and booklets handed out on the street like bread about to go stale; words didn't mean as much as the action they were calling to produce. Language meant nothing if it didn't *do*. Action, being an activist, came from words. With words, he lashed out at his commanders, his disdain of those who stayed silent, who marched mutely through the barracks. The only words they uttered rolled down the command chain from their tongues, ordering those with no power, with no *say*, up to cargo planes where they were shipped in darkness halfway around the world, the first time they would ever leave their state, their country. Words used in the classroom by his peers who had money to travel by other means, who had been to Rome and Athens and Switzerland, but had enough money not to go to Vietnam. Their moneyed phrases hung heavy in classrooms, inadvertent confessions of their shirking duty. Studying literature was an escape for the wealthy from a reality too horrifying to imagine. In those years, words were elbows used to make space in those tight barracks, crowded streets—elbows used against those who wanted to lower him back into his space. Behind his desk, a sign said, **STOP THE WAR**, written with a blue Sharpie, an unwelcome sign for the other officers who came to his desk to throw another file on it. A sergeant came one day and barked at him to take it off. He obeyed, removing the brown Sellotape from the wall. Returning to his book, he found it hard to make out the Cyrillic words. Just then, as he lifted his face from the book, he realized for the first time since he was stationed there that the room had no window.

For my eighth birthday, I got a portable cassette player. Perhaps my parents were tired of me taking the dining chair, getting up to the hi-fi system, and filling the room with music when they were trying to take a nap. Or maybe it was that, at eight, there was nothing in my life that wasn't music. I tore open the cardboard box and uncovered a small, silver rectangle with black holes for speakers. Then, batteries were stored on one of the shelves in my father's large, concave studio, tucked in with the glass, wooden pallets, rocks, and tools. I wanted to be the one to get the batteries, but I couldn't, because I was barefoot and shards of glass were strewn all over. At eight, there was nothing that wasn't music—and nothing but art. I truly believed that all grownups were artists: all men had large, concave studios where they would listen to the radio or have friends come over to sip mint tea with leaves picked straight from the garden and served in cracked porcelain cups that they found at the flea market at the end of the day when vendors just wanted to get rid of their merchandise. All the men I knew were artists, and all the old women chain-smoked long-stemmed menthol cigarettes and cursed and gave out stale candies. I believed everybody was a painter or an actor, sculptor, and potter, because those were all my friends' parents and all the people I knew, or my parents knew, which meant I knew them by association. There were people who weren't artists, but they didn't live in our village, besides my best friend's father, who was a dentist—but all places need a person to fix people's teeth.

Just two years before, graduation day: a sea of silver buttons pressed against uniforms, young eyes hidden under caps. Standing at attention, the cadets listened to the keynote speaker, who *some forty-odd years ago, stood where you're standing right now.* He talked about finding strength by believing in family, in the unit, in the army, in our great nation, permanent things every cadet could build his world around. However, my father, at twenty-one, could not ignore that the world the cadets were stepping out into, at the beginning of the summer after the Summer of Love, was changing rapidly. There was a chasm forming. He could feel the tremors under his polished military shoes; maybe the tremor was inside him because he, a second lieutenant in the United States Army, a fresh West Point alum, on the first step of his lifelong army march, didn't know what side of the divide he'd end up on. He wanted to be a scholar, not a swordsman, yet a sword was fastened to his hip. What world was worse fighting for? Or against? The cadets clapped and threw their white caps in the air high, high, until they plunged down, like planes falling from the sky.

I was attached to my portable cassette player via earphones everywhere I went: my friend's treehouse, walks in the forest, the playground where my friends and I would play football until the older kids came with their basketball and shooed us away. I had never seen a record store. My musical repertoire was based on the weekly music TV show playing Madonna and Madness, Machina, and Fortis. Before every show, I would get a blank cassette my parents would buy for me when shopping in the city or after my father taught at the art school and placed it next to the TV speaker. Whenever there was a song I liked, I hit RECORD, excited to hear the song on my cassette player after the show. But I didn't like many songs, because that music felt fleeting compared to my parents' collection. Their cassettes, titles written in cursive English I could barely understand, had in them sounds of worlds and times so bigger and different than the small one I lived in that every cassette felt like a universe unfolding in song. Kids at school would laugh at us for listening to folk and jazz and rock and swing, old-little kids placed out of time, preferring Peter, Paul, and Mary over Guns N' Roses, but I was content in those little universes of sound. One day, I was walking around the village. Oren, a guitar player who was our neighbor's lover and lived in a ramshackle cabin in the woods—who was the epitome of everything I, at age nine, wanted to be—saw me walking with my portable player. He smiled and told me, *You should never listen to music when you're walking around, because you'll miss out on the sounds of life*, and walked up the hill. That night, I threw my earphones away and vowed to keep my ears open always.

At twenty-one, after graduating from West Point fifth in his class, my father was sent to Germany to study Russian and teach English. He spent eight months in Geilenkirchen, a NATO no man's land at the westernmost part of West Germany. The West couldn't feel more East: Europe vomited millions from its stomach, including my great-grandparents, battling the currents of the pogrom tides arriving at Ellis Island, on that westernmost riverbank of the world. There, they shed their old, travel-weary clothes, along with their old language. My grandfather, who was born in the Bronx—the place named after the river—never knew Russian. In World War II, he served in Alaska, looking to the West in case there was a Soviet invasion. He was on guard for people who spoke his father's tongue. My father, for eight months, sat in class, reciting after the teacher: *"Doma* (дома); *otets* (отец) *home, father."* His forgotten grandfather's tongue was taught on the grounds from where Jews were swept away eastward and drowned in the camps of Bergen Belsen, Buchenwald, Warschau, Sobibor, Lodz, Lublin; in the killing field of Babi Yar; in the town of Nyzhyn, which my father's family escaped all those decades ago. Geilenkirchen was a delta of history, and my father felt its overpowering currents. Nightmares began to plague him: he's running through a dense forest wearing a faded, striped uniform. He's weak and malnourished, but he keeps going. He can hear dogs barking; German guards are running after them. He can hear them murmur, over and over: *Sapad* (запад), *Vostok* (восток), West, East.

Nyzhyn, a town in central Ukraine, famed for its illustrious alum Gogol, (his nose, along with other parts of his face, are memorialized at the town's square), was a place of rebirth for my father's family. My father's great-great grandfather, who was from the outskirts of Moscow, perhaps, whose last name was Rabinovich (the name that would become the Jewish stock character in Soviet humor, full of wit and wile) perhaps,—no one really knows—was, along with other lower class Jews living under The Russian Empire, were to serve 25 years in Nikolai I's—the Russian Haman—army (those who had money could buy their way out of the martial life sentence). His generation would be cannon fodder on the battlefield of the North Caucasus, in the forests of northern Europe, the first to greet, with bullets and bayonets, Napoleon's army. He may have found it odd, my unnamed ancestor, that he had to serve under a tsar who despised his people, fight for a place fought against him. In act of survival—or subconscious resistance—my forefather fled at the dead of night, leaving everything behind—including his last name. The placeless person eventually got to Nyzhyn where he had relatives and took the name of the place. However, to be from a place, to assume its name, can only take root after one is no longer there. The family flowed southward and ended up in Odessa and were known as the family from Nyzhyn. My father heard tales about his forefathers from his grandfather. No, they were not drinking tea with Bialik, our national poet, nor spitting fervor about the cause of Zionism. His grandfather swore that the stories were immortalized in Babel's Odessa Tales, those about horse thieves and other vagrants living in the outskirts of the port city. They lived with their ears open always and could hear the coming sounds sticks being dragged on the ground and rifles being cocked. They could feel the ground's tremor caused by millions of footsteps of people coming east, east, to get on a boat that would take them west; the thuds of horses of those in pursuit of them, who in an ecstatic orgy of violence swept towns and villages all around the empire, events that inscribed the soil with blood, on which Bialik wrote his most famous epic poem *In the City of Slaughter*. They felt this seismic wave and decided to take to sea. They set sail from Odessa to the United States with no objectives but to be nameless, to sink into blissful anonymity which the new continent promised. They may have rejoiced upon seeing New York but perhaps, they may have looked upon the strange city on the sea, the first piece of land they would have seen in weeks and, feigning a smile of relief to the other passengers, their heart would swell with lament because of the beloved city on the sea they left behind. Emigration is not about seeking future fortune but leaving existing failure. It is surrender as much as it is hope: no one leaves their home if they have a name. *Lieutenant Nechin*, The Sergeant Major called my father by his Ellis Island warped surname. *Your request has been approved. You may apply to universities to enter the Russian Language department.* In a few months he would be leaving Germany on a cargo plane headed to California. Upon flying over New York, my father might've been sleeping, dreaming of homecoming in Russian.

The bus would come pick us up every morning for school, a twenty-minute drive from the village. We never knew if it had picked up kids from one of the agricultural settlements surrounding our village. If we were first on the bus, we would run to the back seat and get into defensive position to block other kids from sitting next to us. If there were other kids on the bus already, tensions would rise quickly. A plastic bottle would sail through the air, with gobs of spit, shouts, and shrieks. It was automatic, a morning ritual reminding us of our geography, of who we were not. It was only where we were from that defined us, the artists' village. I didn't know what it meant exactly, to be an artist or to think close to the heart of things, but I knew its value as labor. Art wasn't exalted. It was bread. Its makers were simply laborers, as some of the artists in the village were. (Selling art was never discussed. Or maybe I was too young to tune my ear to the fluctuations of the art market.) All I knew was that everyone who was an artist made our village possible. There was some world view that was common. But on the bus, we the kids of the artists' village, all twelve of us, ages ranging from seven to thirteen, were everything that was opposite to their world. Fighting was the only bond we shared.

When Men Talk To Me

Mary Boo Anderson

I see endless red
Zig-zag lines
under all of their words

I live in new york
I've been "busy"

I'm killing unkillable plants

Plants are so passive aggressive
Like 'i'm wilting and thirsty
But also i'm Fine'

I need all living things to communicate clearly
W me

Ppl always think that by not being clear
They're being nice
They're softening the blow

Bitch what blow
Bitch tell me your expectations and needs
So i can lovingly fulfill them or fuck off

Sorry I Couldn't Make It I Was Busy Rotting

All of these grand plans
And instead I'm fighting
Over the temperature of a room
That I'm no longer in

Selected Tweets

- Being alive is just microdosing death lol
- Short term goal: drink 8 glasses of water a day
  Long term goal: drown
- Motivational poster that says "You miss 100% of the shots you don't take" in an AA meeting room
- Random guy hitting on me wasn't taking my hints to go away so I made my voice as deep as I could & said "pls stop talking to my girlfriend" & ive never seen anyone leave faster
- Boy are u the MTA bc u keep saying you're improving but ur still terrible
- A group of cops is called a murder
- Any little thing someone does to make you happy is a big thing
- I got banned from tinder bc my profile was the green m&m
- Instead of getting hobbies I just get more annoying
- Brooklyn runs out of oat milk, people resort to milking their tote bags for nondairy drink w the most cultural capital per ounce
- I'm like MoviePass in that I'm risky, don't make any sense & will ultimately disappoint everyone
- Wasting my potential? I prefer to call it subverting expectations
- Grimes dating Elon makes her even more relatable to me bc I too have dated some seriously evil men for seemingly no reason
- You can call me sugar as long as you know that I too will eventually kill you
- self-care in the form of muting all my exes
- I don't trust online recipes that have a novel before u get to the actual ingredients
- Pretty sure my roommate is using a pooper scooper to drain pasta & idk what to do about it

- I don't believe in god but I know a lot of goddesses
- I assume everyone's in love w me until they slash my tires and even then I'm like hmmm maybe they just don't want me to leave them
- Why do poets like coke? Because of the line breaks
- What does satan call her ovaries? Deviled eggs I'm sorry
- I want to be the hype man for everyone I love
- My parents must think im adobe flash bc they never keep me updated
- Every twosome is a threesome if you disassociate
- Honestly even hell knows im miserable now
- All apps are dating apps if you're online enough
- Third base is posting a pic of them on Instagram
- The little engine that could but probably won't
- Every season is cuffin' season in the prison-industrial complex
- If guilty feet have got no rhythm maybe that's why white people can't dance

Cave
(Excerpt from a short story)

Daphne Palasi Andreades

Marcia got a taste of the primal relations between bodies—of those relations that lay unspoken yet vibrated at the surface, an electric erotic undertow—she got a taste of this phenomenon one evening as a waitress.

Marcia had recently moved to Cebu, one of the Philippine port cities teeming with street market vendors, fishermen, college students, drug peddlers, snorkelers, and girls like Marcia, who'd migrated from Luzon's northern provinces. She was from Barlig and was seventeen. In Cebu, the heat awakened plants aggressive in color, size, and density, plants that flourished in the humidity and the fat raindrops which fell, unrelenting, for fifteen-minute stretches, but felt like sixty whenever she found herself caught in a downpour.

She waitressed at The Pearl, a seafood restaurant in the center of Cebu City. She'd been working at The Pearl for two months, serving mojitos and margaritas to tourists from America, France, Britain, and Australia, as well as wealthy Filipinos from the capital. She handed them drinks decorated with flimsy umbrellas, tiny versions of the ones that blighted the beach.

There had been a man at the restaurant. A Filipino sailor. Marcia could smell the chemicals he used to keep his uniform sparkling white. And although Marcia knew what existed between bodies, she'd never experienced it herself. Not love—no, not love—but sex. Though she wasn't a virgin and had slept with one boy in her hometown, a boy who left for the Lepanto Mines and died in an accident when the tunnel collapsed on him, she'd never experienced the kind of desire that emanated from the sailor. Five rounds of whiskey had helped Marcia say yes. Clumsily, she tucked away the money he'd slipped her, one thousand pisos, into the pocket of her dress.

She assumed they would go back to his hotel, and so, was surprised when he led her through a side door and up a dim flight of stairs. He opened an unmarked room. Inside, a bed was pushed to the corner and a salmon-colored curtain shielded the outside world from Marcia's bare breasts.

Though drunk, Marcia knew that is was sex, and not love, that tied her to the man. She understood that it was her lips and ass and tongue he desired, nothing more. She knew that she didn't love him, of course—She didn't even know him, not that knowing was a prerequisite to love. Before dawn, he tipped her another five hundred pisos. She was stunned. More than the money, Marcia learned a valuable lesson, one that would mark her time in Cebu: she learned her beauty and youth could be used as tools. She'd use them, she decided, like the plow her father wielded to uproot ripe crops.

Soberbia

James Cañón

Evening was falling and the station was still packed with vendors offering fried foods and small plastic bags filled with purified water. Soberbia and Lucy got off the bus, each carrying a backpack, and together they broke through the crowd toward the exit. Outside, they made small talk for a short while. They learned that both were visitors and that they had no relatives or friends awaiting them. Neither one dared ask the other's—nor disclose her own—reasons for traveling to such a remote town on Christmas Eve.

Soberbia imagined that Lucy was a naïve gringa traveling alone through Colombia, thinking she was defying stereotypes while wearing a ridiculous fanny pack. But at least she did not seem particularly crazy or dangerous.

Meanwhile Lucy decided that Soberbia was a young man transitioning into a young woman, and that he or she had either run away from home or been kicked out for being different. But at least he or she did not seem particularly crazy or dangerous.

Soberbia suggested they look for an affordable boarding house, and then stepped aside to ask recommendations from a street vendor. Meanwhile, two large women in big skirts and a boy holding an ice cream cone stood next to Lucy. The boy immediately began throwing a tantrum and, in what appeared to be an accident, dropped his ice cream down the front of Lucy's T-shirt. One of the women yelled at the boy. She quickly produced a handkerchief from her bosom and without asking began to rub it on Lucy's T-shirt. Lucy stepped back, baffled, but then the second woman came into the scene, apologizing and helping the first one to clean Lucy's T-shirt. When Soberbia heard the commotion she at once recognized the fraudulent scheme. She hurried over to the scene and grabbed the two women by their necks. "Give it back, you bitches!" she yelled, assuming the voice and demeanor of a rough man. The women returned to Lucy the cash they had taken from her fanny pack, then quickly disappeared into the crowd.

"Are you alright?" Soberbia asked Lucy, her voice female-like again.

"Uh-huh," Lucy said, unconvinced and confused. The robbery attempt had shocked her, but what really puzzled her at the moment was Soberbia's sexuality. She might not be a man transitioning into a woman after all, but rather a man disguised as a woman for a reason other than pleasure or amusement. Maybe he had done it to escape from mandatory military service. Or perhaps he was a delinquent trying to avoid capture.

"Let's get out of here," Soberbia said, pushing her enormous sunglasses up on her nose. "I've found us a decent boarding house." She put her arm around Lucy's shoulder and together they started down the street.

The boarding house was A two-story building, or rather a one-and-a-half story building for the upper level was an abandoned shell of faded orange bricks without windows, fixtures or fittings. It was clear that the owner had run out of money before completing the construction. The lower level, though finished, also looked grim on the outside. But the inside of the house was surprisingly charming and cozy. Both the living room and the dining room were visible from the wide entrance. They were divided by a large desk shaped as a "U," which served as a reception area. The living area was modestly furnished with wicker sofas and chairs, brass-colored lamps and a wooden coffee table with a stained top, and it was equipped with a large 1970s console TV standing on four thick legs, like a pig. The dining area had a long table with ten mismatched chairs neatly arranged around it. A hideous artificial flower arrangement sat in the middle of the table, which was covered with a white tablecloth with a herringbone pattern. On the wall behind the dining table there was a handwritten list of the "Don'ts" of local dining etiquette, which included, among other things, *Don't pass gas at the table, and Don't wipe your mouth with the tablecloth.*

"I'm afraid I only have one room available," said the owner, sitting at her desk with her nose in her logbook. "It's next to the kitchen and it's rather small but it has a full-size bed." She was in her late forties and had a wrinkled forehead that contrasted with the smoothness of the rest of her face. "It's perfect for two people; that is if you don't mind sharing the bed." She waited a few seconds and then, addressing Lucy, said, "I'll give it to you for ten thousand pesos a night; half what I normally charge. And that includes breakfast for both of you!"

"We'll take it," Soberbia said to the owner before Lucy could open her mouth. Then she told Lucy, in a soft voice, that she only had a large bill. Would Lucy mind paying for both of them? She would pay Lucy back later.

The room was the size of a closet and smelled musty. In the days before refrigerators it might have been a kitchen larder. It was also dark despite the white paint on the walls. A small aperture in one of the walls was meant to function as a window, but it looked into a dark hallway, admitting neither light nor air. On the opposite wall hung a frameless mirror that had been charged with the responsibility of somehow making the space look bigger, but the room was so small that it made the mirror look larger than it was. The bed, covered with a polyester floral quilt, and a freestanding coat rack were the only pieces of furniture in it. Nothing else would have fit.

Lucy looked dissatisfied but she did not say anything. She was more troubled by the thought of having to sleep in the same bed with a cross-dressed stranger. They laid their backpacks on the bed and Lucy went to use the bathroom, which was outside, at the end of the hall, and was to be shared with guests from five other rooms. When she came back into their room, she found Soberbia sitting on the bed with her sunglasses perched on her head like a headband, applying powder foundation on a black and blue bruise around her left eye.

"Ouch! Does that hurt?" She said, trying to sound casual.

"It only hurts my good looks." Soberbia closed the foundation container and put it inside her backpack. "Are you hungry?"

"I'm starving," said Lucy. "I haven't eaten anything since this morning."

"Let's go then." She reared up and quickly adjusted the sunglasses back on her face.

"I...I think that we should talk first," Lucy said timidly.

"What about?"

"About...who I am and who you are. We should know a little more about each other if we're going to sleep in the same bed. Don't you think?"

"What is it you want to know?"

"Well...say, for instance, what kind of...woman or man are you?"

Soberbia gave a long sigh. Then, abruptly, she pulled her skirt up to her waist with one hand and yanked her underwear down to the middle of her thighs with the other. "This kind," she said in a sharp, irreverent tone. Lucy gasped and her hands flew to cover her mouth, but her eyes remained fixed on Soberbia's crotch. She had no penis. Only a severe scar, wrinkled up like burnt plastic, remained where her penis had once been, suggesting the amputation had lacked in compassion. Her testicles, however, were where they should be, and they appeared to be intact. Lucy looked the other way, suddenly feeling uncomfortable and ashamed. Soberbia pulled her underwear up, and giving Lucy a naughty grin, said, "I showed you mine, now show me yours."

Lucy raised her eyebrows, said, "How can you joke about this?"

"Oh, relax," Soberbia retorted. "It's been three years. Besides, he did me a favor."

"Who? Who did this to you?"

Soberbia started to answer but changed her mind. Instead she said, "I'm really hungry. Can we talk about this later?"

Disappointment Is All I Get For Free

Naomi Falk & Mina Hamedi

N: On the commencing day of this month's period, as I was digging my fists into my pelvic muscles and rolling my fists at other people's gods, it occurred to me that each cycle of my bleeding comes with the understanding that I am nearly older than my mother was when she gave birth to me.

M: Scars and marks seemingly fade from the body, but I don't believe this to be the absolute truth. The skin, the muscles, the bones, they absorb everything. Every scratch and impression becomes a part of you. You carry them with you the next morning, covering the red and purple, the raised skin, in the armor of your choosing.

N: And in bleeding, I lose part of myself, something I search for until realizing it is gone and that it will never return. It is the case that we are constantly turning into something new, acquiring and shedding. Mina says we come together and fall apart.

M: She goes through this all the time. Am I the same person when the sun rises the next morning? Is she? The blood gets thicker, the marks deeper. Sometimes, that is what we want.

N: To say a woman is diminished by these things that change her would be an egregious error. And how to know if I slept and awoke as the same person if I reached my hand over to the pillow beside mine in the slant of morning light and found that there was no one there?

I only dreamt there was a witness.

M: And if there is someone to reach for; blankets in waves, four pillows that never end up where they began, how much of me is left behind after each metamorphosis? How much have you taken in return? I'm not sure there is a simple, "me," anymore. I surrendered her a while ago.

N: In surrendering her, I abandoned my will to contain the feverish landscape of my mind to the confines of my body. I am hungry to be the thought that punctuates his days. I snake my arms around his ribcage in the middle of the night and press my face into his spine until I see stars before my eyelids. I gaze into the saintly realm beyond the moon.

M: Bodies are elastic to everything we ask and seek of them. I'm losing sight of the lines that distinguish where I begin and he ends. I'm told, over and over, to exist in the present. Maybe I can only do this when there are no layers left to discover, to destroy.

N: But it could never be the case that you will become unexplorable to me when you breathe more expansively than all the windows in this corridor down which I stride. Recite any minute that has composed your life and I kneel before the altar.

M: You remember details I used to pride myself on being able to recall first. The way a gaze becomes fixed or broken. How everyone has their own way of sliding fingers through hair. I am trapped by my thoughts, too. Sometimes they escape: a fist against the wall or clawing at empty spaces.

N: The transcension of thought into impulsive action is like an old friend by now, though I somehow remain surprised at the shadows I cast over a future I have no choice but to approach. Sometimes I wonder at the insignificant and uncontrollable circumstances that, in retrospect, define the shape of our lives. What might the other versions of me have thought about someone like me?

M: I dream of another world where words spoken in the ecstasy of anger never hurt. I don't belong to the same home an ocean away or the same blood ties. My tethers vary. I can stay in my room forever, quenched by the lights down the avenue, the harsh sunsets and sanguine daybreak. I can see the world as my mother does, not focusing on the little pains of every day.

N: Our atmospheres shift us into new designs. Daytime's isolation leaves us wondering what it is that we've missed while we were consciously slumbering through the lunchtimes and the morning commute. The world turns into the beyond as we adopt the palette of midnight. On snowy sidewalks made fleshy by neon and fluorescence, we'll stumble down the street ceaselessly flashing cameras in each other's faces, texting all our friends as we wonder how they, too, might be faring in this nocturnal kind of life.

M: We have our vigils. The sounds we play that make us come alive, the smoke wafting up toward exposed lightbulbs, that familiar taste in small glasses. If even for a few seconds that night, all versions of ourselves move as shadows do. But I don't sleep. I close my eyes and wait for a few hours to pass. This exhaustion, there is no reprieve. Oh, but we love it.

N: There was a moment in which I turned around and did not recognize her, my best friend. I saw her moving as a stranger, a undefinable form in the orbish haze of emerald in the room. Here was a life so affected by my own. And as I say it now, it is hard to imagine it happening, to have seen myself as a stranger from the familiarity of my own skin.

M: I pull apart the stitching of those I love and seal myself inside. I walk my best friend's path to work, I taste the water, feel fingers on paper, legs aching with greater strides. The faces talk back at me. Perhaps I feel the keys of a piano, guitar strings, the soft fur of an imprudent cat. I quiet the voices down. Then I emerge and lay beside them.

N: Beside them in this room, this room in which I am endlessly alone with them but cradled by them.

M: Maybe we are not done yet at this time and place. With this changing and shedding. Maybe, there is more to collect.

N: I want to believe that the course of life is a continuum, that what I've lost along the way can still belong to me.

M: If I can hold onto even the smallest piece, the nights will be enough, the scars will remain but they will not hurt, and you will tell your stories the way I've been telling you mine.

John Farris

With his sharp wit and abrasive personality, the poet, novelist, playwright, raconteur and artist John Farris, who died in 2016 at age 75, was for decades an integral part of the Downtown literary and jazz scenes.

He performed his poems and prose anywhere on the Lower East Side that would have him. He was a friend of David Hammons and Sun Ra, a mentor to Paul Beatty and Darius James, a bodyguard of Malcolm X's, a perpetual rent-free roommate, including to Ornette Coleman, and a fixture at a variety of bars, drinking for free, talking shit and getting kicked out.

Though he was constantly writing, Farris would quickly alienate anyone in a position to publish his work—only in 2010 did he publish his only novel, *The Ass's Tale*, and his poetry is limited to one short book from the 1990's and a few appearances in journals and anthologies.

Yet his influence extends far beyond what ended up in print.

Here are a few pieces from the book of his *Last Poems*—which is as yet unpublished.

Angle

Angle. You are
always after
some angle. Same ol'
angle: talk about a blast-
you can't even have
it straight

One Night

One night
I dropped my
eraser down
the toilet.
Shit I said,
shit. A
friend said
that's what I produce
anyway. All
my friends, all my relatives
are so doggone
predictable no
matter who
or what I have here (talk
about your pipes, your misfits), everything I own
out of sight even
with my
constitution
Talk about inspiring!
Talk about
your culture,
(your caste).

My Word

I give my word
freely: it doesn't cost much
for me to keep plus
its no fun. Imagine
a word kept quiet.
If I had one it would mean plenty
less than George, by George George-
George, did you get that?
How is that for inspiration,
a fine lyric, a hymn
What does it mean translated
if not the same thing?
Shoes are shoes. Hank's neck
turning, otherwise
what's the point. I'm afraid
there is. It's like
new music. It's like
when your lover has
not gone. It's like not entertaining
the basics. It's like me
inventing blue
and swinging it.

Critique

I draw badly
well; neighbors
noses, frowns lips,
eyes, shoulders
much too
narrow for
the chest on
Breasts & bellies, hands
are what
drew me
into this. Knuckles
& joints of
all kinds. I get a blade
Here- a bone
There. A flight
Of birds headed south
To somewhere
Take a leg,
A head, a
Bike leaned
Against a magnolia.
Garbage. If
grunts were given out
for that I'd be as rich as
David Hammons,
Maybe. I'd get a car, paper, chow.

Lore

Kenkeleba House abuts El Reverendo
Pedro Pietri Way: the bard of Kenkeleba House
sits high in a turret in his castle
mixing excrement for what: "a
little piss makes green," he says, "I only like
the good shit, for the blues
I listen to Miles Davis, Shirley Scott, Gilly Coggins,
and Frank.
Looking out that window.
He says pointing to where the
El Reverendo Pedro Pietri Way is changing me
makes me see red, and more red, it's too much. I'd
put that song
behind the eight ball if I could, but he's dead.
"My hair is white. Around here," he says. /the purple
plainly apoplectic
"I'm the institution. Get me?" When it comes to
whirling squares
and Fibonacci, I'm Monet,- I'm Monet!"

Moves in Time

Steve Anwyll

To say he stands as high as my chest would be a lie. And his club-foot makes him even less intimidating. But his eyes are nothing more than little black balls of hate. And I'm not sure what offence I've committed. Because it's clear he has it out for me.

But there I go again. Being suspicious. It must be all the marijuanna. So to clear my mind of plots against me I glance up the block. I see a woman walking. Instantly I'm hooked. She looks nice. Dressed well. In a manner out of style for decades. Her long skirt moves in time with her hips.

And even though I can't see any of her features that doesn't stop me from fantasizing about my fingertips tracing imaginary lines on her cool raised flesh. Her begging me to fuck her. And a pint of my hot cum spraying all over her tits while we both laugh hysterically.

I'm getting worked up as she gets a green light. She struts through the crosswalk with confidence burning like a bonfire. I remind myself it's rude to stare. So I look at the ground. The click of her heels getting closer is deafening.

Then there they are. On the sidewalk in front of me. Blood red leather. High polish. My heart races. I raise my eyes. The hem of a long pleated skirt. Blouse. Fitted jacket. Flowing dark hair.

When we make eye contact she asks me so quickly in French to purchase a smoke that I almost miss the light mustache. The sharp jaw. *Ceci n'est pas un cigarette madame*, I reply poorly. Gesturing to the smoldering joint between my fingers.

She laughs.

And I regret I gave up the habit.

I watch her walk away while returning to my fatasies. But that's when the little fucker blind-sights me. His whole body darts out like a punch. Full force shoulder hits in my stomach. I fall to the sidewalk. Close my eyes. And listen to his giddy laughter as I pretend his club-foot ain't swinging at my face.

Ligament

Christopher Gonzalez

They are flopping over one another, faces grinding against legs and thighs, arms reaching for the support of a headboard, the mattress. I am backing away, pressed hard against a popcorn-textured wall—their sweaty bodies are all my camera can see.

Together they are shifting, sliding. Just like you and I, from before.

They invited me to film this sex tape, to capture what most sex tapes ignore: All the intimate bits, the unexplored close-ups. The dampness of her hair, for one, how it clings to her cheeks in streaks of bold red. And his body, no longer nervous, the hypnotic flexing of his hairless calf muscles. The intensity in his eyes; the veins in her feet, wilting beneath the surface when she closes her toes around a nest of twisted sheets.

Our last time together, I had wrapped my arms around you in bed, your back a wall of solid heat against my chest. I wanted to melt into you, to fuse together with a ligament in your spine and keep you upright, aligned.

He is tracing her lips with his tongue, now, inching his way down her neck, dotting her chest in delicate beads of saliva, each of them sparkling for a second before the golden light of the camera washes them away. She is worrying his earlobe between her pointer and thumb, rolling a prayer into his skin like putty and hoping, I imagine, it seeps into his soul.

They are stroking along, lapping each other up with mutual hunger. I am waiting for a gap to blow open between them. When he comes, I pan across their hot pink bodies, blotchy beneath a curtain of sweat.

The room reeks of fucking. There is a smile in both of their eyes, and it stays there as I approach them, the camera hanging down at my side, the lens now capped.

I often wish to hit pause on these films, to start over. A mid-action rewind. I wish to scan the corners of each frame for a hand, maybe a strand of hair, or a stray thread of fabric, or the glint of a broken engagement ring—any sign of you dipping into the scene, there and gone, like a quick greeting, to let me know it's all O.K., it's not what I think, that you never really disappeared.

They are hesitant at first; such cold hands touching my back. My request is an odd one, but I assure them this is what I need. I am hunched forward over the edge of the bed, waiting for them dig into me with a blade, to root around in the meat of me. I asked them to unbury my spine and pop out the vertebrae, until all the parts of me I could never see are stacked at the foot of the bed, pulpy and stringy, greasy with fluids, glaring up at me, this perfect mound of all that I am.

∞.
End of time
(Excerpt from *Hellscape*)

Chris Molnar

The sun had been expanding for many years, and the only life form left on Earth was Strain 121, a single-celled microbe, one of the original organisms to emerge seven billion years beforehand, when the Earth had come together. A few hundred million years before the oceans had evaporated, beginning an era of bright moist silence, as the carbon dioxide that could have let this greenhouse host life had long since escaped. The great boiling valleys and mountains had ceased to move, the thick gaseous spray hanging without wind, floating slowly upwards. Strain 121 had stayed under the sea when microbes were migrating to the surface, staying close to the undersea peaks venting the unutterable heat of the planet's core, trapped and molten things from times more ancient than even the single cells of Strain 121. With the ocean at first lifting in pressure and then vanishing, the communities around the vents, not more than six or seven altogether, spread by tectonics over the Pacific and Southern Oceans, had rapidly gone through stages of hibernation, cellular division, and primitive movement, not straying far from the oxides that fed them, but trying to understand this new world in their way.

With the whole world at their disposal, they spread out once again in a brief window of a million years before the temperature would rise beyond even their noble fortitude. In these million years, Strain 121 recaptured what had been theirs at the birth of the planet—an undulating ball of cosmic debris now coming apart. Even without waves, over thousands of years they began to reenact the journey that their brethren-cells had once undertaken seven billion years before, crawling over ridges and across deserts, to the abraded Himalaya or the crushed brick and metal of Manhattan.

But the sun drew nearer, implacably, and the even the darkest night, when the Earth's hopelessly corrupted axis would spin unusually far away, would be bright, a blunt pastel purplewhite insistent through the ever-lifting fog. Still distant from finally enveloping the tired planet, the white dwarf sent pulses toward it, and one pulse, of a century-long duration, surrounded Earth, siphoning all remaining atmosphere, and within the first few years the last cells of Strain 121, not far off what in another world was the North Atlantic Coast, pro-tected by a landslide, existing in a molten cave, biostatic and sleeping, were consumed.

ARTISTS AND WRITERS

Mary Boo Anderson is an artist and writer living in Brooklyn.

Daphne Palasi Andreades is from Queens, NY. She is an MFA Fiction candidate at Columbia University, where she received the 2018 Henfield Prize. Her heroes include Zadie Smith and Cardi B, among others.

Steve Anwyll is the author of *Welfare* (Tyrant Books, 2019) and lives in Montréal.

Hratch Arbach was born in Damascus, to a Syrian father and an Armenian mother. He moved to Paris in 2000. he received his Ph.D. in microbiology and virology from the University Paris VII. He then joined one of the leading Paris-based Art school, l'Ecole Nationale Superieure des Arts Decoratifs. He works with different media, including photography, painting, drawing and scenography. The key element of his work is the state of man from past to present and he constantly seek to push the boundaries of our consciousness on the way to unification.

Arash Azizi is a writer, translator and scholar living in New York City. His writings and commentary on politics, history and cinema have appeared in numerous publications including the *BBC*, *The Daily Beast*, *Jacobin*, *Al-Monitor*, *The Atlantic Council*, the *Toronto Star*, *Vanity Fair*, *The Washington Post*, and *Al-Jazeera*. As a doctoral student in New York University, he researches the history of transnational links that bound Iran and the Arab World to each other in the framework of the broader Global Cold War. About a dozen of his book-length translations have appeared in Iran and abroad.

James Cañón was born and raised in Colombia. He received an MFA from Columbia University. His debut novel, *Tales from the Town of Widows & Chronicles from the Land of Men* (HarperCollins, 2007), has been translated into eleven languages and published in over twenty countries, and was made into a film. It was also selected as one of the "Ten Best Books of the Year" by the *American School Library Journal*. James has been the recipient of numerous awards, including the Prix du Premier Meilleur Roman Étranger, and the Prix des Lecteurs de Vincennes. His short stories and essays have appeared in many literary journals and anthologies in the US, Mexico, France, Belgium and Colombia. He teaches at Columbia University.

Nifath Karim Chowdhury lives in New York City.

Jessica Denzer is a writer and educator. She received her BA in English Literature from Fordham University and her MFA in fiction from Sarah Lawrence College. She is a researcher in residence at the New York Public Library and writes fiction and nonfiction. Her work has appeared in *Number Magazine*, and she is a contributing editor and writer for *Four Way Review*. She lives in Brooklyn, NY.

Naomi Falk lives in Bushwick. Her writing fixates on art, intimacy, and the ways in which we engage and disconnect our sensory perceptions. She works at The Museum of Modern Art, is the Editorial Director of Ki Smith Gallery, and is co-founder of NAUSIKÂE NYC.

John Farris was a poet, novelist, playwright, raconteur and artist who was integral for decades in the Downtown literary and jazz scenes. Before he died in 2015, at age 75, he published only the novel *The Ass' Tale* (Autonomedia, 2010) (which won a PEN Oakland award in 2011) and the poetry collection *It's Not About Time* (Fly By Night,

1993). His *Last Poems*, co-edited by Chris Molnar and Nicodemus Nicoludis, are forthcoming from Archway Editions.

Jameson Fitzpatrick is the author of the chapbooks *Morrisroe: Erasures* (89plus/ LUMA Publications, 2014) and *Mr. &* (Indolent Books, 2018), and the collection *Pricks in the Tapestry* (Birds LLC, 2020). Recent work has appeared or is forthcoming in *The New Yorker*, *The American Poetry Review*, *The Believer*, *Cosmonauts Avenue*, *Poetry*, and elsewhere.

Caitlin Forst is a writer and bookseller living in Brooklyn.

Jean Kyoung Frazier has an MFA in Fiction from Columbia University, and the author of *Pizza Girl* (Doubleday, 2020).

Christopher Gonzalez serves as a fiction editor at *Barrelhouse* and a contributing editor at *Split Lip*. His stories appear or are forthcoming in a number of journals, including *Lunch Ticket*, *Wasafiri*, *Third Point Press*, *Cosmonauts Avenue*, *Pithead Chapel*, and *The Acentos Review*. He was the recipient of the 2015 Ann E. Imbrie Prize for Excellence in Fiction Writing from Vassar College. Cleveland-raised, he now lives and writes in Brooklyn, NY and spends most of his free time on Twitter: @livesinpages. You can also find him online at www.chris-gonzalez.com.

Evan Gorzeman is a writer from Long Beach, California. He received an MFA from Columbia University and lives in Brooklyn where he is working on his first novel.

Mina Hamedi moved to Manhattan from Istanbul in 2010. Her work attempts to unearth the things that bind dreamspace and reality and to understand what defines an individual's relationship to family.

She is an agent at Janklow & Nesbit Associates and co-founder of NAUSIKÂE NYC.

Brent Kite's writing has appeared in publications including *The Believer*, *Barrow Street*, *Film Comment*, *Sight & Sound*, and *Trafic*, as well as the anthologies *Exile Cinema* (SUNY, 2008), edited by Michael Atkinson, and *Olivier Assayas* (Austrian Film Museum, 2012), edited by Kent Jones.

Jason Koo is the author of three full-length collections of poetry: *More Than Mere Light* (Prelude, 2018), *America's Favorite Poem* (C&R, 2014) and *Man on Extremely Small Island* (C&R, 2009). He is also the author of the chapbook *Sunset Park* (Frontier Slumber, 2017) and co-editor of the *Brooklyn Poets Anthology* (Brooklyn Arts Press, 2017). An associate teaching professor of English at Quinnipiac University, Koo is the founder and executive director of Brooklyn Poets and creator of the Bridge (poetsbridge.org). He lives in Brooklyn.

Noah LeBien is a graduate of Shimer College and received a MFA from Bennington College. Published in *Prelude*, *Crab Fat Magazine*, *Uppagus*, and others. Currently living in Brooklyn.

Anya Lewis-Meeks is a writer from Kingston, Jamaica who lives in New York City. She was a participant of the 2016 Callaloo Creative Writing Workshop at Brown University. She is an MFA candidate at Columbia, where she teaches University Writing. She is at work on two novels—one set at a Jamaican high school, and the other at a fictional Ivy League college. She has published fiction in *Panorama Journal* and *Winter Tangerine*. She is also a reader and editor at *Apogee Journal*.

Chris Molnar is an author, co-founder of the Writer's Block bookstore in Las Vegas and editorial director of Archway Editions.

Etan Nechin is an Israeli-born journalist, author, and online editor for *The Bare Life Review*, a journal of immigrant and refugee literature.

Nicodemus Nicoludis is a poet, adjunct and bookseller living in Queens, NY. He is the author of the chapbook *Natural History* (Rot House Books, 2018) and his work can be found in *Yes, Poetry, Reality Hands*, and elsewhere. He is the founding editor of Archway Editions.

Kate Olsson is a bookseller living in Brooklyn. She has a BFA in Writing from Pratt Institute. Her work has previously appeared or is forthcoming in *Hobart* and *Selfish Magazine*.

Erin Taylor is an American writer based in Brooklyn. You can read her work at erintaylorisalive.com and tweet at her @erinisaway.

Joanna C. Valente is a human who lives in Brooklyn, New York. They are the author of *Sirs & Madams* (Aldrich Press, 2014), *The Gods Are Dead* (Deadly Chaps Press, 2015), *Marys of the Sea* (Operating System, 2017), *Sexting Ghosts* (Unknown Press, 2018), *Xenos* (Agape Editions, 2016), and the editor of *A Shadow Map: Writing by Survivors of Sexual Assault* (CCM, 2017).

ACKNOWLEDGMENTS

Thank you to Mark Meneses for organizational help, and Mina Hamedi for the idea to publish this anthology.

CREDITS

Gas Stations at Night (Wild Radio 1) can be found online at vimeo.com/121398052

Artifacts of the Moon (Wild Radio 2) can be found online at vimeo.com/224871645

"Morning, Motherfucker" by Jason Koo reprinted with permission from *More Than Mere Light* (Prelude Books, 2018)

Videos by Hratch Arbach can be found at www.hratcharbach.com